KINGDOM

By C. WASH

Are You On Our Email List?

Sign Up On Our Website

www.thecartelpublications.com

Check Out Other Titles By The Cartel Publications

Shyt List 1: Be Careful Who You Cross
Shyt List 2: Loose Cannon
Shyt List 3: And A Child Shall Leave Them
Shyt List 4: Children Of The Wronged
Shyt List 5: Smokin' Crazies The Finale'
Pitbulls In A Skirt 1
Pitbulls In A Skirt 2
Pitbulls In A Skirt 3: The Rise Of Lil C
Pitbulls In A Skirt 4: Killer Klan
Pitbulls In A Skirt 5: The Fall From Grace
Poison 1
Poison 2
Victoria's Secret
Hell Razor Honeys 1
Hell Razor Honeys 2
Black And Ugly
Black And Ugly As Ever
Miss Wayne & The Queens Of DC
Black And The Ugliest
A Hustler's Son
A Hustler's Son 2
The Face That Launched A Thousand Bullets
Year Of The Crackmom
The Unusual Suspects
La Familia Divided
Raunchy
Raunchy 2: Mad's Love
Raunchy 3: Jayden's Passion
Mad Maxxx: Children Of The Catacombs (Extra Raunchy)
Kali: Raunchy Relived; The Miller Family
Reversed
Quita's DayScare Center
Quita's DayScare Center 2
Dead Heads
Drunk & Hot Girls
Pretty Kings
Pretty Kings 2: Scarlett's Fever
Pretty Kings 3: Denim's Blues
Pretty Kings 4: Race's Rage
Hersband Material
Upscale Kittens
Wake & Bake Boys
Young & Dumb
Young & Dumb: Vyce's Getback
Tranny 911
Tranny 911: Dixie's Rise
First Comes Love, Then Comes Murder
Luxury Tax
The Lying King
Crazy Kind Of Love
Silence Of The Nine
Silence Of The Nine II: Let There Be Blood
Silence Of The Nine III

By C. Wash

- Prison Throne
- Goon
- Hoetic Justice
- And They Call Me God
- The Ungrateful Bastards
- Lipstick Dom
- A School Of Dolls
- Skeezers
- Skeezers 2
- You Kissed Me Now I Own You
- Nefarious
- Redbone 3: The Rise Of The Fold
- The Fold
- Clown Niggas
- The One You Shouldn't Trust
- Cold As Ice
- The Whore The Wind Blew My Way
- She Brings The Worst Kind
- The House That Crack Built
- The House That Crack Built 2: Russo & Amina
- The House That Crack Built 3: Reggie & Tamika
- The House That Crack Built 4: Reggie & Amina
- Level Up
- Villains: It's Savage Season
- Gay For My Bae
- War
- War 2
- War 3
- War 4
- War 5
- War 6
- War 7
- Madjesty vs. Jayden: Short Story
- You Left Me No Choice
- Truce: A War Saga (War 8)
- Truce 2: The War Of The Lou's (War 9)
- An Ace And Walid Very, Very Bad Christmas (War 10)
- Truce 3: Sins Of The Fathers (War 11)
- Truce 4: The Finale (War 12)
- Ask The Streets For Mercy
- Treason
- Treason 2
- Hersband Material 2
- The Gods Of Everything Else (War 13)
- The Gods Of Everything Else 2 (War 14)
- Treason 3
- An Ugly Girl's Diary
- The Gods Of Everything Else 3 (War 15)
- An Ugly Girl's Diary 2
- King Dom
- The End. How To Write A Bestselling Novel In 30 Days

WWW.THECARTELPUBLICATIONS.COM

KING DOM

By

C. WASH

Copyright © 2023 by The Cartel Publications. All rights reserved.
No part of this book may be reproduced in any form without permission
from the author, except by reviewer who may quote passages
to be printed in a newspaper or magazine.

PUBLISHER'S NOTE:
This book is a work of fiction. Names, characters, businesses,
Organizations, places, events and incidents are the product of the
Author's imagination or are used fictionally. Any resemblance of
Actual persons, living or dead, events, or locales are entirely coincidental.

Library of Congress Control Number: 2023902265

ISBN 10: 1948373912

ISBN 13: 978-1948373913

Cover Design: T. STYLES

First Edition

Printed in the United States of America

What's Good Twisted Babies,

I'm back to share some incredible news with all of you. It's time to introduce my baby's latest creation, *"KING DOM"*!

"KING DOM" is a true gem that will resonate with everyone, but it holds a special place for the dominant women out there. In a world where it can be intimidating to know and fight for your authentic self, Charisse has crafted a masterpiece that captures the essence of that struggle.

I have to take a moment to express how incredibly proud I am of Charisse. She poured her heart and soul into *"KING DOM,"* showcasing a character whose raw vulnerability speaks to all of us trying to figure shit out.

Now, let's shift our focus and keep in line with tradition. In this novel, we want to give a well-deserved shout out to the phenomenal cast of:

A HUSTLER'S SON

These extraordinary individuals have left an

By C. WASH

indelible mark, both on and off the screen. Their performances are nothing short of amazing, and Charisse and I can't contain our excitement as we prepare to introduce them to the world this summer.

Get ready for a riveting experience that will leave you wanting more. So, take a seat, relax, and prepare yourself for the captivating journey that awaits you in "KING DOM."

Let's Go!
T. Styles ☺
President & CEO
The Cartel Publications
www.thecartelpublications.com
www.facebook.com/authortstyles
Instagram: Authortstyles
www.twitter.com/cartelbooks
www.facebook.com/cartelpublications
www.theelitewritersacademy.com
Follow us on IG: Cartelpublications
Follow our Movies on IG: Cartelurbancinema
#CartelPublications
#UrbanFiction
#PrayForCece
#AHustlersSonMovie

#KINGDOM

By C. WASH

PROLOGUE

The dusk spread its crimson wings over Northeast Washington DC. '99 was the year that Felicio King, barely fifteen, was locked lips with her secret flame, Gina Light. Sitting in an old broken down 1976 Chevy Nova they hid, tucked away behind Mrs. Johnson's run-down house.

The crib, the car and Mrs. Johnson were all on their last legs, so Felicio felt it was the perfect space and opportunity to try and get hers.

She removed her Catholic School Uni the moment the bell rang and she bolted out the door to meet her crush at "the place". Currently showcasing a t-shirt and her father's oversized Washington Wizards basketball shorts. She wore the items underneath her uniform always to make herself feel better about having to wear the dumb ass skirt and blouse.

As Maxwell's, 'Fortunate', boomed from her portable silver dual CD and Cassette player in the front seat, Felicio was trying to convince Gina to let her suck on them titties in the back seat.

"Noo, girl, if I let you, you'll tell somebody." Gina whined.

"No I wouldn't. If I did, you ain't gonna let me in no more." Felicio begged.

She covered her lips again with her own knowing that this was the key to open Gina's legs.

"Mmmm...Mmmm," She moaned as Felicio continued to enjoy the way her Strawberry lip gloss tasted and knew it wouldn't be long before she could start to feel her up.

It was time to go further.

Do better.

So, Felicio tried her hand.

She lifted up Gina's school blouse and exposed her white cotton bra.

Excited to be advancing, she pawed at her budding breasts while still kissing her deeply, but she wanted more.

Felicio slowly moved her hand underneath her skirt, up her thigh and straight to her panties.

"Don't tell, promise?" Gina whispered.

"Promise." Felicio replied with a smirk.

She knew she was in there now!

With all systems pointing to go, Felicio placed her fingers in her underwear and into her pussy. She was surprised at how wet Gina was since this was their first time together.

But being inexperienced, Felicio was now stuck.

She always envisioned and anticipated getting to this moment, yet never thought about what to do next.

But she wanted her badly.

So she decided to let instincts take over.

She paid close attention to when she focused on a certain area, how Gina began to move her waist and grind against her hand. Felicio made sure not to move her position once that happened.

This is all she had been waiting for, she was so sised to be in this car with her girl having this experience.

She glided her finger in and out of her snug opening as she slipped her other hand down into her own draws to satisfy the intense yearning she felt. She closed her eyes and gave into the moment with Gina, but then came trouble.

The Nova's back door was snatched open, and Felicio was yanked up out the pussy by her ponytail.

Gina's older brother, Duke, was having none of it and came to spoil the fun.

"King! What the fuck I tell you about staying away from my sister?! Huh?!" He yelled at her while she swung wildly trying to free herself from his grasp.

"Get off her, boy! We weren't even doing nothing, just talking." Gina yelled.

"Oh, yeah...then why the fuck your shirt all out of place and these windows fogged up?" He asked, glaring her way.

Gina pulled her blouse down and adjusted her uniform skirt not realizing how she looked when she stepped out the car.

"She telling the truth. We was just talking and listening to music. Now get the fuck off me, Duke!" Felicio pleaded.

While keeping a strong hold on her hair, he grabbed one of Felicio's hands and sniffed her fingers.

Uh oh!

"You a lying ass dyke bitch! You was in there finger fucking my little sister!" He yelled gripping her ponytail tighter. "I'ma kill you!"

"Duke, please just let her go." Gina begged.

He brought Felicio's head close up to his face. "If I catch you around my sister again I'ma treat you like the nigga you tryin' to be and crack you in your fuckin' jaw."

He let go of her hair and smooched her down by her forehead. She stumbled back catching herself before she fell.

Suddenly, the screen door on the back of the house swung out and Mrs. Johnson came charging out of it carrying a bat. "I told y'all motherfuckas to stay out my got damn yard!"

Because she weighed about 400 pounds her charge was more like an angry waddle, slow and unbalanced.

Duke and Gina took the opportunity to take off before she got anywhere near them. But Felicio's boombox and bookbag was still in the Nova.

She was trapped.

"Felicio King," She yelled out of breath when she got to her. "I'm calling your father! Come in this house. Now!"

"Fuck!" She whispered under her breath. This was the last thing she wanted.

Although Mrs. Johnson's house looked fucked up on the outside, it was surprisingly cozy inside.

It was neat, clean, and smelled of cinnamon and fresh baked apple pie. But Felicio was scared as shit.

Calling her father was the worst-case scenario. She would've rather been hit by the bat.

With the yellow plastic handset fixed to the wall crushed in her grasp, she said, "Mr. King, this is Mrs. Johnson, I caught your daughter and another little girl doing God knows what in my car out back. I'm sick of chasing her and the rest of these horny mothafuckas outta my yard. Now I'm five minutes from calling the police!" She yelled into the yellow receiver. "What you want me to do with it?"

Felicio's heart rocked.

This was worse than death.

Her father sighed. "No ma'am, that won't be necessary, I'm on the way."

She slammed it down and folded her arms over her chest.

30 MINUTES LATER

Normally, Felicio loved riding in her father's 1993 Fleetwood Cadillac as it floated around the streets of DC.

It was burgundy with a cream top and cream interior. That bitch was sexy, and she couldn't wait to have a car that fly when she got older.

But today, when it pulled up to the curb outside of Mrs. Johnson's house, she wished she didn't have to get in it.

As she sat in silence looking out the window at the stores they passed, she couldn't help but wonder how she would be punished for this.

"Why you wearing my shorts, Felicio? Where's your uniform?" Her father asked, breaking the silence.

"Ummm...The boys pull on the girls' skirts sometimes in school and I wanted to have something underneath mine if it happened to me. My uniform is in my bookbag." She lied praying he bought it.

"So a boy trying to get at you but you in the backseat of a bucket with a girl?"

"We were just listening to music."

He shook his head and pulled down the ashtray compartment containing the cigarette lighter from underneath his radio. He pushed the lighter in to heat it up. Next, he removed the jack he had tucked behind his ear and placed it in his mouth.

When the lighter indicated its heat, he retrieved it and applied the fiery end to his cigarette, igniting it. After putting the lighter away, he took a drag from the jack. "You going to my sister's house for three days."

Felicio hung her head.

Her aunt's house was not the place she wanted to be. It was cramped, dirty and there was never enough food to eat.

Her aunt had five kids, her cousins, and she didn't get along with any of them niggas.

"Daddy, I'm sorry."

"So am I."

Her head hung low as he dropped her off with nothing but her boombox and her bookbag. Her aunt, who was in her fifties, opened the door and let Felicio in.

Before she could close the door behind her, she said, "Listen, my brother said you gotta stay here and I'm gonna let you, but you know the rules. Stay out my kitchen, don't touch my TV or phone and if I have company, make yourself invisible."

Felicio nodded her head reluctantly.

"Oh, and since he said you a dyke now, you won't be sleeping in the room with my girls. Go on down into the basement and sleep on the cot." She instructed.

The steps creaked as she made her way to her new unwelcoming home. It was dank and she got zero rest amidst the dripping walls and the massive ass rat running rampant, tormenting her through the night. The sleep was haunted by its relentless scurrying and squeaking, while invading her dreams with fear and despair.

Felicio was in hell, literally, that's what the basement of her aunt's house felt like.

She had no idea how the fuck she was gonna make it there for one night much less for three. In that moment she vowed that no one would ever make her feel this way again.

Or else.

THREE UNCOMFORTABLE DAYS LATER

Felicio was excited about getting back home and into her own bed. When her father didn't show up, she decided to walk, not wanting to spend another second under her aunt's roof.

She hadn't really eaten in the past couple of days, so she was starving.

Not to mention she didn't have a change of clothes, so she needed a hot shower and some grub a.s.a.p.

When she arrived at her house, she was shocked to see it was dark inside. Normally at this time, the front porch light would be on and so would most of the lights.

Why was it different?

She trotted up to her door and turned the knob.

It was locked.

She reached into her bookbag and pulled out her key, but when she tried to stick it into the doorknob, it wouldn't go in.

"Fuck is wrong with this shit, young?" Felicio said as she took it out and examined it by turning it left to right.

She tried to insert it again, this time she flipped it upside down, hoping that would work.

Nope!

She looked around, her dad's car wasn't outside which meant he wasn't home but why couldn't she get in?

Deciding to leave the key shit alone, she walked around to the side of the house.

Her pops didn't know it, but when she was late and wanted to sneak in, she climbed through the side window and avoided waking him up. She purposely kept the window unlocked so that she always had a way in if she needed one and just as she hoped, it was open.

She carefully popped the screen out and used her palms to slide the window up. Once it was halfway open, she hoisted her body inside.

But when she got in, she was shocked at what she saw.

Wall to Wall nothing!

No couch in the living room, no table in the kitchen, even the oven and the refrigerator were gone.

"Did somebody rob us?" Felicio thought as she suddenly became fearful.

She climbed back out the window with haste and ran across the street to her neighbor's house.

Banging on the door, her heart pounded like a pocket beat at a Go-Go!

"What the hell are you knocking so hard for, girl!?" Her neighbor Mrs. Turner asked, opening the door.

"Sorry, I think we got robbed. Can I use your phone, I may have to call the police 'cause my dad's not home." She explained pulling for breath.

"Child y'all ain't get robbed, I saw your father moving out two days ago."

Her stomach flipped and she felt like she had to shit.

"Huh...moved out...wh..what you mean?" She asked, confused.

"What don't you understand? He moved...saw him carrying boxes and furniture out to a truck that he hitched his Cadi to and drove off." She explained. "White landlord was here earlier today changing the locks. I thought your manly ass was with him."

"That's why my key ain't work." Felicio said mainly to herself.

"Look, I'm watching my stories! I recorded them while I was at work, and I been waiting to see 'em all day. Now, don't be banging on my door like you crazy no more." She yelled before she slammed the door in her face.

Felicio was devastated.

She trudged back across the street and climbed into the window again.

As she walked around her empty house, tears streamed down her face. Why would her father move without her?

The hurt she experienced took over her body as she slid down the wall and onto the floor where she cried herself to sleep.

By C. WASH

CHAPTER ONE
WE OUTSIDE IN THE CLUB
PRESENT DAY

Thirty-nine-year-old Felicio strolled through the throng of club-goers, her head held high as fuck, moving like she was king of the world.

April Montgomery, her thirty-year-old roommate, and friend, tried to get her attention but she couldn't be bothered.

The night was young.

And the bitches were sexy.

Felicio, a commanding presence in the spot, towered above the crowd. Her tall, statuesque figure moved with confidence and grace, as if she owned the dance floor.

The neon lights reflected off her light skin, highlighting the intricate artwork that adorned her body. From her face, neck, arms and even down to her legs, vibrant tattoos weaved like a comic book, each design telling a story of her journey.

"Hey, Felicio," one of her 'in the past-smash's' said, fingertips waving her way.

She winked but continued her stroll.

She had her before.

It was time to try something new.

She exuded a striking, masculine energy that drew all eyes to her. Her locs, neatly braided into two French braids, represented a crown of rebellion and self-expression.

Her gear screamed power and confidence because everything she donned was handpicked and held meaning.

Tonight's fresh garments included a form-fitting black leather jacket, unzipped to reveal a tank top that hugged her toned physique. Her skinny ripped jeans gripped her legs, accentuating her slender figure.

A king was nothing without her crown jewels, right?

So, adorning her neck were several gold and diamond chains, glimmering under the club lights, signifying her status while also snatching souls.

In her hand, she held a glass filled with Don Julio, the ice cubes clinking softly against the sides as she swayed to the rhythm. The drink served as a symbol of her control and indulgence, a taste of the luxurious lifestyle she had carved out for herself.

Just like the ladies wanted a piece, April, her roommate, watched her with the same lustful gaze. Afterall, she had a secret that she wanted to share that night. And it was that she was and would forever be in love with her, despite Felicio not being with the shits.

Besides, she wasn't Felicio's brand.

April was 5'11" tall and had a thicker body type. Her physique resembled that of a wrestler. Broad up top and slimmer down toward her lower torso.

She was what one would call a soft Dom. Not all the way Fem and not all the way Dom. She was jive somewhere in between and Felicio could or would never understand.

She wore her hair in a short curly cut that was shaved around her temples, a curly temple taper.

"Don't walk over to her," April said to herself. "Just leave her alone."

She did everything she could to hold herself back, but she felt as if now was the perfect time. So she tipped over to her, interrupting her flow. "Hey, Felicio, can I talk to you 'bout something?" April raised her voice to be heard over the loud music. Lips closer to Felicio's ear than she liked.

"What up?" Felicio snapped, barely even glancing in April's direction. Besides, a cutie had just passed her view with a dress so tight she saw the cleavage of her ass cheeks clap with each step.

"I...I feel like...um."

Felicio looked at her to be sure all was well. "What is it? You good?"

"Yeah...I just..." Drunk off the last three shots, slowly she moved in for a kiss.

"Fuck is you doing!" Felicio snapped, a stiff arm in the center of her chest.

"I...I wanted to—."

"What's wrong with you, bro?"

"Nothing...I—."

"Because it looked like you was 'bout to kiss me." Felicio screwed up her face as if she smelled something foul.

April was beyond embarrassed. If she could have burrowed herself into the floor, she would have done it with the quickness.

It was time to flip the script.

"Nah...Uh..I wanted to rap to you 'bout new business I've been working on. It's foot modeling...online. I think it could really be lit and bring in some good money for the fam."

Felicio smirked and rolled her eyes.

"I'm sick of you with this shit! What, you think you gonna make us rich by showing niggas your feet over the internet or something? That's dumb as fuck." She laughed. "We've got bigger things happening for us other than your little wanna be side hustle. Told you that already."

April was taken aback by Felicio's dismissive attitude.

"It's not a little side hustle, Felicio. It's a legit business, and I think it could really get us right."

Felicio turned to face her fully, her eyes narrowed. "You think you know what's best for the fam? 'Cause you don't." She pointed a finger in her chest. "You new, April. I built this from the ground up, and I know what's best for us. Niggas wanna be high. Niggas wanna forget the shit they got going on. Ain't nobody trying to see no funky feet in the—"

"Watch how you talk to me."

Felicio's eyes narrowed. "Is that a threat?"

"Should it be?" April stood her ground.

Felicio knew she could make her cry, so she paused. "This ain't the time. I got this family. Always have. Always will."

"I'm not saying you don't. But I think it's worth considering. We could use the extra income, and it doesn't hurt to explore new opportunities. Right?"

Felicio shook her head.

"Ain't got time for this, slim. I've got more important shit to worry about. Like that fine ass bitch with the pink paint dress on in the corner. Later for all this extra shit." Felicio walked off and disappeared on the hunt, leaving April standing alone, frustrated.

Felicio stood tall in front of a table, a cup of champagne now in her hand, as the other members of her squad gathered around her. That included April as well as thirty-three-year-old Zora Henderson and thirty-one-year-old Khari Williams.

Zora, queer and considered a bad bitch stood, 5'7" with brown skin. She was thin but had a cute shape and rocked long box braids that continued to swing out of her face the whole night. But sis kept them baby hairs neatly laid giving very much Janet, Poetic Justice, tease. She was loud and quick tempered, but very smart and extremely loyal.

Khari, on the other hand, was completely the opposite. She considered herself bi-sexual but a bad bitch in her own right. And that was no lie. She was no taller than a minute at 5'2", thick with nice curves. She was a neat freak who suffered from Sickle Cell Anemia.

They didn't just party together, they got money together.

Lived together.

And fought together.

The club, full of bammas and noise, rocked by the Go-Go music in the background, but Felicio's voice cut through it all.

"I just wanted to take a moment to say how much I love y'all niggas," she said, raising her plastic cup in a toast. "Y'all my fam, my support system, my everything."

The others raised their cups in return, murmuring their agreement.

"I know we've been through some tough spots lately," Felicio continued, her voice growing more serious. "But I want y'all to know that we in this together. We have each other's backs, no matter what."

April rolled her eyes and took a premature sip. Still hurt off the rejection. "I hear you," she said dryly.

Felicio took notice of her behavior, then turned to Zora because she wasn't worth the energy.

"And Z, you know you special to me. The one who keeps me grounded, who always reminds me why we doing this in the first place."

Zora blushed, feeling a wave of love wash over her. "I'm just doing what I can to help you, Felicio." She retorted with seduction in her eyes. "To help us."

Khari, the only other member of the group, sat in anticipation and admiration of Felicio.

"Let's raise our drinks, to us," Felicio said, rims pointed to the ceiling. "To our family, to our future!"

The others raised their cups higher in unison, echoing Felicio's words. "To our family, to our future."

The music thumped on, the club full of energy and life.

The evening was winding down, but Felicio was still collecting numbers.

She was standing near the bar, dancing with Khari and Zora when they heard raised voices over the music coming from across the room. They turned to see April, standing toe to toe with a stranger, her fists clenched at her sides.

"Fuck is going on over there?" Felicio squinted, her voice sharp.

The women followed her gaze, their eyes widening in alarm. "I don't know, but we need to go see what's happening," Khari said, stepping forward.

Felicio with Khari behind her, pushed their way through the crowd to get a better view. They could see April, her eyes flashing with anger, as she faced off against a guy who looked to be dumb drunk.

"You really embarrassing yourself out here, man!" April said, her voice rising. "What is your fucking problem?"

The stranger, a tall, slender man, sneered at her with narrowed eyes. "You my problem! You should be—"

Felicio immediately stepped between them, her eyes blazing. "My dude, you need to back off." She said, looking dead in his face as if she were forewarning him. Her voice was low and dangerous. "Fuck is you doing in a gay club anyway?"

The man looked at Felicio, then laughed. "Who you think you are?"

Felicio squared her body up in front of him. "Look, you probably had a lot to drink and wandered into the wrong situation. Maybe you should just call it a night and find your people."

"Fuck you! You don't run shit." The man yelled at Felicio before looking her up and down. "And you definitely don't run me." He said with a smirk.

A crowd began to hover around them.

Felicio glanced to her left and to her right. She noticed how her girls were looking on with faces of *say word and we jumping him.*

"Listen, man, we out here enjoying ourselves, we don't want no problems." Felicio told him calmly. "For you."

"And I don't want no problems either! What I want is for—"

April shoved the man hard toward the exit.

After he regained his balance, he charged at her.

Now he'd done too much.

Felicio didn't hesitate. She swung, hitting him in the jaw and he stumbled back, his eyes widening in surprise.

He grabbed his jaw and looked around.

Rage looked like it entered his body and took over as his brain tried to put together what just happened.

"You must have lost your mind!" He yelled now charging toward Felicio.

Just as the shit was about to really kick off, Zora came flying into the melee with a broken Champagne bottle preparing to cut the guy new slits all over his face. Her arm was high in the sky ready to kill when one of several bouncers grabbed her by the wrist.

"Easy, pretty lady," he said with the other arm around her waist. "You doing too much now."

The other bouncers yanked up every last one of them.

Drunk dude included.

Within minutes, they were all carried to the front door and tossed outside like New York City trash.

The air crackled with tension as the four friends, Felicio, April, Zora, and Khari, stood outside the club they had just been tossed out of. Their hearts raced, adrenaline pumping through their veins, still shaken from the recent altercation.

Who was the nigga who assaulted April?

And why?

As he continued to get his ass whooped by the guards, the nigga was still belligerent as he was taken further away front the property.

Felicio and her group stood there, still breathing hard and staring at each other in shock.

They had never been tossed out of a club before even though from all the fights they caused they gave plenty of reasons.

"Y'all threw us out when you can clearly see that nigga was the problem!" Zora yelled at the security guards who stopped what they were doing and looked over at the troublemakers.

"Get the fuck out of here!" One of the guards said, as the stranger was taken further away from the club and the foursome.

"Who was he?" Khari asked April.

"I already said I don't know," April replied, annoyed.

"Let's go home," Felicio added as she looked at April once more. Digging into her pocket she pulled out her phone and looked at all of them. "Plus I got Pink Paint's number already."

Zora and Khari laughed.

"Your sex drive crazy as fuck," Khari chuckled.

"You would fuck anybody," Zora added.

"Nah, not anybody." She put her arms around their shoulders, while April followed, head hung low.

CHAPTER TWO
CRIB SHIT

Khari and Zora sat in the backseat as Felicio lay asleep in the passenger side of April's truck. April stared over at her every few minutes in a way that made things awkward had anybody bothered to notice.

She wanted her.

Never wanted a person more badly.

And the things April did to get her to choose her, from their beginning, made her dangerous.

But nobody had a clue how dangerous, slim could be.

"We here, Felicio," April said after parking in front of their apartment building. When she didn't nudge awake, she used the opportunity to touch her. With the palm of her hand on Felicio's arm, her fingers touched the side of her breast. "Bro, it's time to get up."

Felicio's eyes opened and April drew her hand back quickly.

"Yeah, get the fuck up," Khari and Zora yelled from the back. "The party ain't over!"

Khari and Zora, still drunk boots, climbed the steps as Felicio pulled herself out with April's "extra attentive" help.

When they entered their crib, it was like a breath of fresh air.

The spot, right in the heart of Northwest, DC had them feeling blessed. It was their own little oasis, embodying the vibes they loved.

This place wasn't just your average apartment— it was a dope-ass crib, representing their love for hip-hop culture. Graffiti-style artwork adorned the walls, paying homage to the icons who paved the way. It was something like a visual mixtape, telling their story loud and proud.

The living room served as the crib's heartbeat, blending comfort and swag. Big-ass sectional couches with fly throw pillows, beckoned them to kick back and vibe which they did often.

And that flat screen?

It was begging for marathon sessions of binge-worthy shows.

Their vinyl collection held it down, meticulously displayed on a sleek shelf. It was like a museum of sound, spotlighting the full spectrum of the culture. From the classic artist of the past, right down to the new and bold like, Lola Brookes.

Now, the kitchen—was where the magic, gossip and shit talking happened.

And, thanks to Zora, each bedroom had its own vibe, reflecting the unique personalities of its occupants.

They weren't even in the apartment before shoes were kicked off, damp jackets were tossed on the floor and purses flung at the door. Khari, the resentful cleaner, walked behind them organizing their mess.

"Damn, that nigga ruined it for us," Zora said as soon as her sweaty but sexy ass hit the couch.

April rolled her eyes. "Can you leave it the fuck alone? Please?"

"Why you getting all uptight?" Khari said, tossing the pile of junk neatly into what she called the baggage claim.

"Ain't nobody getting uptight."

"All I'm saying is that before that shit broke out, I was talking to this dom that–."

"Already fucked everybody in the club." April said interrupting. Eyeing the front door, she focused on Felicio who was peeling her clothes off one item at a time and leaving them in a pile on the floor near her bare feet. "You need help over there?"

Felicio shook her head. "I ain't busted, if that's what you getting at, Champ."

Ever since the pandemic, she didn't believe in wearing her outside clothes inside the house. Not to mention anywhere near her bed.

She never understood how folks could come home and jump into bed wearing the same shit they had on outside.

And, if she went home with a broad and they moved like that, she would kindly pack up her "dick" and roll.

It was a no for her, period.

When she was in boxers and a t-shirt, Khari picked up her items and put them in baggage claim with all the other shit.

"How come I'm not feeling your answer?" Zora said.

"Whether you feeling it or not, from this point on, you talking to yourself," April added.

"Like you be half the time?" Khari laughed with Zora's help.

Zora unzipped her knee boots and pulled them off her feet.

Zora favored all things heels and when she put them on, she could go from 5' 7" to 5' 9" easily.

She could have any nigga she wanted, if that's what she wanted, but it wasn't. She was a Fem who loved women.

All women, no particular type, just adored the softness of their bodies next to her own. Whether Dom or Fem, she ain't care as long as they looked good and had good energy.

That was a requirement.

Oh, and they couldn't be goofy...Her spirit couldn't handle goofy shit.

Khari was different.

Fem, her beauty was understated but still shone through naturally. She wore her hair short in big finger waves. She too was a lesbian but preferred only dominant women.

For the most part she was quiet but far from a pushover.

Felicio met all three of her roommates online through an app called *Lots of Piscine.*

Since she was abandoned by her family from her late teen years to present, she decided one day she would build her own. And after spending time over a stretch of months with each woman, her *Kingdom* was formed.

The only contingency was that, if they chose to live there, they had to pull their weight in the family business.

Currently, the family business was selling prescription pills that Felicio got from her plug.

Each of them was responsible for selling their shares.

They kept a percentage of the money they made, and the rest of the profit went to Felicio. For the most part, she used it to take care of all the bills in the apartment and to re-up when needed. Felicio, Zora and Khari had an understanding. Although she met them initially with the idea of being in a relationship, they realized they were better as, family with benefits.

It was April who couldn't get with the program.

Tiring of Zora fishing, Felicio strolled toward the bar on the other side of the couch and grabbed the *Gran Coramino* tequila and held it up.

"It's shot o'clock! Who taking one with me?"

Zora was the first one on her feet and stood next to Felicio.

Khari took her blue YSL bag off her shoulder and walked toward the bar for her glass.

April, who was low key relieved that Felicio changed the subject, followed suit.

Felicio handed each woman a glass and proceeded to fill it with two fingers worth of tequila.

"To my niggas, Salud!" Felicio stated before downing her shot.

"Salud!" Everyone else shouted.

Felicio poured herself another, slammed the glass down and then asked, "So...who in a nigga's bed tonight?"

April's eyes got wide with hopes of being picked.

"Ohhhhhhh...so now you come crawling back our way, huh?" Zora asked, teasing Felicio.

She shook her head, "I had pink body dress in my sights for tonight but..."

All eyes fell on April who's situation fucked the night up.

She looked at Zora and Khari. "...I can show y'all what I was gonna do."

April sighed and threw back her shot before saying, "Fuck y'all, man."

Felicio had the main bedroom in the apartment.

It was sleek as a bitch and built seduction tough.

As you stepped into the room, a sense of warmth and intimacy washed over you, inviting you to surrender to its sexiness.

Smack in the middle of it all, a majestic King-sized bed stood, commanding attention. It was accented with plush, inviting pillows, and draped in a luxurious fur comforter that beckoned you to sink into its softness.

To keep the mood, she had blackout curtains surrounding the room in a cocoon of privacy. Controlled by a sleek ass remote, the curtains could be effortlessly drawn closed, shutting out the world and creating an intimate sanctuary.

One of the two and a half bathrooms in there was connected to Felicio's room, which provided an additional touch of luxury and privacy for all her late-night fuck sessions.

And tonight was no different.

After Felicio got cleaned up, she was joined in her room by both Zora and Khari who were showered, lotioned and scented.

It wasn't unusual for the threesome to take place. Shit, in this apartment, they shared everything, even each other.

There was only one exception, under no circumstances did Felicio get down with April.

But she wasn't selfish, and this wasn't about being in love, so if Zora or Khari wanted to get with April without Felicio, she ain't give a fuck.

But they never did.

They were all free to do who and what they wanted.

She was a Dom who kept her sex partners at an arm's length. And she believed in being very transparent with each of them.

They needed to know up front that she would not be with them exclusively and warned them about falling in love with her.

If they did, it wouldn't shake out well in the end because she had no problem cutting them off.

The only light in the bedroom came from several candles Felicio had sparked on her dresser.

She lay in the middle of her bed with nothing on but a fresh black sports bra and her special boxer briefs.

They were briefs with a rimmed hole in the front for her strap that would fit snugly inside.

She loved using her "dick" at playtime but couldn't stand using a traditional harness. All them buckles and straps got the fuck on her nerves.

Her briefs made it feel like she could pull her joint right out of the boxers and the rim held it securely enough to fuck her girls down, with ease.

She went all out for her dildo too. Even ordered a "pack and play" strap.

This type of joint was what a lot of trans men purchased as their dicks because of how real it felt. It cost a grip, as it was handmade, so that every single detail made it look and feel just like the real thing. She was even able to pick out the color that matched against her own complexion.

She put real thought into her "dick" and took pride in pulling it out when the time was right.

And, at the moment, the time was perfect.

Summer Walker's *Just Might* boomed through the speakers that flanked the closet doors.

Zora, ass naked, crawled up onto the bed first and positioned her freshly waxed pussy directly over Felicio's mouth.

It wasn't a whole lotta foreplay needed with her, she liked to get straight to it.

But this was a group affair and Felicio wanted to take her time with this shit. So, she cupped her butt cheeks and lifted her up and down to make sure her tongue was positioned directly under Zora's clit.

She wasn't licking just to be licking, she really enjoyed the taste of pussy, and she treated it as a delicacy.

Felicio slid her tongue inside of her tunnel and then moved her mouth up to suck on her button gently. She knew this drove her crazy.

Zora's body was heating up with ecstasy and caused her to move her waist back and forth to fully ride Felicio's face.

"Mmmmmmmm, damn that shit feels so good, don't stop." She threw her head back and said.

Felicio continued to swirl her tongue rapidly over her clit making sure to catch any juices that slid out.

"Shit, Felicio," Zora whispered, reaching down to grab her hair while whining her hips, moments away from exploding.

Khari, not wanting to be left out the party, also climbed onto the bed. However, 'cause she was much shorter, she needed a couple of attempts to actually hop up onto the platform.

But, she made it work, and when she got up there, she concentrated on Felicio's lower body.

On her knees she crawled up to her waist and freed her joint from out of the boxer briefs.

It stood upright with a bit of a bend as if she were semi-erect.

Knowing how Felicio liked to get down, Khari began to lick the shaft of the dildo.

Now, we all know Felicio couldn't feel it, but that was of no consequence. In her mind, she was getting head and she got into it properly.

"Yeah, suck that shit." She said with her tongue still deep in Zora's pussy.

Khari went to work licking the extension of Felicio with precision and passion and when she couldn't take it anymore, she straddled her and placed the dildo snugly inside of her own drenched tunnel.

The scene was steamy, highly erotic but far from over.

In another bedroom, bored of playing with her own clit, April wanted to join the fuck session that was going down in Felicio's room. Besides, the moans were so loud, she wondered if they were sending her soft invites through the air.

She contemplated for a while about how she would slide in but then decided to just go for it. "Fuck it, I'm just gonna walk in and get in where I fit in." She said out loud to herself.

She took another shot of tequila, to muster up some courage, and headed into Felicio's room with a slightly moist pussy.

As April quietly turned the knob on the door and slowly crept inside, the only sounds that could be heard were moans and TGT's *FYH*.

She moved in closer and began to take off her tank top and shorts. Just as Khari opened her eyes and momentarily stopped riding Felicio.

"Hold up, what you doing?" She yelled out.

Felicio pushed Zora off her face slightly and craned her neck to see what was happening.

"Bro, the fuck you doing in here?" She yelled at her.

Zora turned her body completely around and sat near Felicio's head on her knees to fully see what the fuss was about.

She was blown that whatever was happening interrupted her pussy from being properly licked down.

"What? I can't join the fun?" April asked, standing at the foot of the bed butt naked.

Felicio was pissed she had to see her in the nude.

"Man, if you don't get your dumb ass the fuck out my room!" She yelled.

"But why? Everybody in here enjoying themselves, why can't I be in here too?" She asked sincerely.

Zora sighed and Khari giggled.

"Because you built like a box!" Felicio yelled louder. "And I told you it'll never be like that! Now bounce!"

"Girl, get out!" Zora yelled.

"Please!" Khari added.

"Ok, well can I stay and just watch?"

Felicio had enough.

She picked up the remote control from off the bed table and threw it in her direction. "Young, get out!"

April ducked down to avoid the remote hurling her way and shuffled out of the room as fast as she could closing the door behind her. She tried desperately not to trip over the shorts that draped around her ankles and when she bent down to pull them up, she noticed that during the shuffle she accidently kicked a pair of Felicio's boxer briefs out the door with her.

Slowly, she bent down to retrieve them from near her feet and held them securely in her hands.

By C. WASH

She looked back to make sure that the door was closed and that no one was behind her. When she knew that the coast was clear, she brought the briefs up to her nose and inhaled them deeply.

CHAPTER THREE
FUCKING HANGOVER

It was the next morning, and the apartment was quiet.

Everybody was in their own room.

Felicio very rarely allowed Zora or Khari to lay with her after they fucked. It was her way of trying to remain in control of the situation and avoid anyone getting attached.

Felicio, now wide awake and completely satisfied from the night before, stretched and reached for the remote to open her curtains.

When she felt around the bed table and didn't come up with the device, she scowled until she remembered why it was missing.

"Dumb ass! The fuck she try to slide in here for?" Felicio rubbed a hand down her face as she recalled how April crept into her room.

She shook the image out her head and got out of bed. Lately April was ramping up her advances, as if she were running out of time and she didn't understand why.

Fuck all that shit. She thought.

She wanted to have a family meeting about the day's business but needed to get everyone up and at 'em. The family liked to party which meant funds were often low and had to grow again if they were gonna continue their lifestyles.

She grabbed her plush gold and black Versace robe off the back of the door and headed to the kitchen on a mission to make niggas rise and shine.

The enticing scent of a bomb ass breakfast feast wafted throughout the apartment, gently coaxing Zora, Khari, and April from their slumber and beds.

As the scent of freshly ground coffee, sizzling bacon, and perfectly cooked cheese eggs floated through the air, their senses came alive, drawing them irresistibly towards the source of the tantalizing aroma.

Zora, her eyes still heavy with sleep and slightly hungover, slowly emerged from her bedroom first. Her nose tingled with anticipation as she rounded the corner into the beautiful modern kitchen. The sight that greeted her made her heart skip a beat.

"Now, this is how you wake a bitch up!" She said heading to pour a cup of coffee.

Felicio, a self-taught culinary artist in her own right, moved smoothly and with purpose around the kitchen.

The smell of her homemade biscuits, fresh out of the oven, filled the room, while a pot of creamy, buttered Old Bay grits bubbled gently on the stove. The mere sight of the golden biscuits, their flaky layers begging to be torn apart, caused Zora's mouth to water in anticipation.

Khari, drawn out by the pleasant fragrance next, followed suit, her steps light and eager. The delicious scent had woven its way into her dreams, and now, reality called her to indulge in the delectable feast.

"Morning, y'all." She managed to say before she took a seat at the dining room table and laid her head down.

It felt like maybe today she'd have to deal with a Sickle Cell flareup which didn't bother her all the time. But when it did it was bad.

Felicio noticed Khari with her head down and approached her with concern.

"Boo, how you feeling?" She asked sincerely. "I ain't break you last night, did I?"

Khari giggled. "You good but not that damn good."

"Lies."

She smiled again and sighed. "I'm ok, it may be a little rough today, but not bad."

"Well, once we're all done here, I'll rub you down to help you feel better." She kissed her on the forehead.

"Thank you, Felicio."

Meanwhile, April lay in her bed staring up at the ceiling. Still feeling dumb from getting shot down in Felicio's bedroom, she contemplated just staying in her room all day.

But she knew her stomach wouldn't allow that to go down. Besides, she would have to face them all eventually. If she went out there now, she could blame it on the a-a-a-a-a alcohol.

Opening the door, she bent the corner and to her surprise, was met with smiles and greetings from Khari and Zora. But she wouldn't be good until Felicio showed that she wasn't mad at her.

When she turned around and noticed April standing there, she gave her a head nod and said, "Sit down, fam. I know you hung over, get some of these grits up in you."

April, now relieved, went to grab a plate.

The kitchen island was adorned with a colorful array of dishes, each one meticulously prepared with love and care by Felicio's skilled hands.

"I knew breakfast would bring y'all niggas right to me." Felicio boasted.

"Hell yeah, I thought I was dreaming but my dreams ain't never smelled that good." Khari lifted her head from the table and chimed in.

Felicio chuckled and bit into her grape jelly covered biscuit before taking a deep sip of coffee.

Needing something cold, Zora walked over to the refrigerator and grabbed the orange juice and a bottle of champagne.

"You didn't get enough last night?" Khari asked, surprised.

"That's why I grabbed it. I got a hangover and the best thing for a hangover is hair of the dog." Zora explained.

"What on earth is hair of—"

"Just a term people say. It means to feel better from a hangover, you gotta take hair from the dog that bit you." Zora schooled while scooping cheese eggs onto her plate.

She handed the champagne bottle to Felicio to be opened.

"But what dog? And how did it bite you?" Khari asked, still lost.

Zora rolled her eyes, "Girl, it just means to get through a hangover drink some more. A beer really helps to even you out, but I don't feel like being bloated."

"Ohhhh, got it." Khari said, a little too loud.

Felicio popped the bottle open and began to pour out the champagne into glasses. She filled them almost to the top and left just enough room for a dribble of orange juice thereby concocting the perfect mimosa.

Still feeling jive embarrassed, April hadn't said a word since she entered the kitchen.

She just pulled back a chair and sat down with her plate, not making eye contact with anyone in the family.

Khari chuckled lightly while chewing on her bacon and grits.

"Before you get lit off these strong ass mimosas, we running low on supply." Zora stated smacking on the food in her mouth.

She was the brains of the family. She managed finances based on the money that Felicio provided. She kept the fridge stocked and cared for their needs.

She was also Felicio's right hand in the business.

Because when Felicio met with the plug and got their product, it was Zora who made connections to distribute. It was she who was able to stay under the radar and find not only people who wanted supply, but who needed it due to many conditions.

Zora was so important that without her shit wouldn't flow.

For the business.

Or for the family.

That power always worried April, and one day she wanted to take it away. No drugs meant no leaning on Zora.

Simple.

"Aight, that brings me to the point of this family breakfast." Felicio announced. "I gotta collect more by tomorrow so I can run past the clinic and reup."

"Ok, I'll bring my end to your room after I finish." Khari said.

"Same." Zora said before downing her mimosa.

"April, you good on yours?" Felicio asked.

"Uh, yeah, yeah, I'm good. Just got a bit of a headache, that's all." April lied. "You want me to go with you? When you re'up?"

"Why would I need that?"

"I'm just trying to help. But I know you going to see Chanel so–."

"Fuck you saying? We see Chanel for—."

"I'm just playing."

"Didn't sound like that."

"Well I am. It ain't your fault the plug is pretty."

"Maybe that headache really is getting to you," Zora said. "'Cause you tripping. Get some of this up in you before Felicio go off." She laughed and placed a glass down in front of her.

"Thanks." She took an unwanted sip since she really didn't have a headache or hangover, and the last thing she wanted to do was drink this morning.

"When will I get your ends?" Felicio questioned.

"Can I give it to you tomorrow?" April asked. She swallowed a lump that formed in her throat.

Felicio took a deep breath followed by a sip of coffee. "Yeah, but no later than tomorrow. I'm hitting the clinic the day after. You got the money, right?"

"Yeah, yeah, just need to go grab it from a spot." April informed.

Zora cut her eyes toward Felicio and Khari.

Everyone continued to eat and drink, and the silence was awkward and obvious.

As they wondered what "a spot" meant?

As breakfast wound down, April cleared her throat, "So I know you said you weren't interested, but I figured since we were drinking heavy last night and everything, maybe you didn't hear all the details accurately. So I wanted to—"

"I know you not 'bout to try and sell me on that feet shit again." Felicio yelled out, cutting her off. "And over breakfast at that."

"But why not though? This is good, safe and legal to do. And the pay can be crazy! We wouldn't even have to leave the apartment." April pleaded.

"Anything to keep King from Chanel." Khari giggled.

"What you just say?" April yelled, slamming a fist down. "

"Just playing," Khari laughed. "I'm not feeling good either."

April rolled her eyes.

"I don't know 'bout you, April, but I like leaving out." Zora chimed in when no one asked.

April side eyed her.

"Bro," She hated when Felicio called her that. "I done already told you, I'm responsible for what this family does to get paid. We been doing 'aight with the pills so ain't no need to switch up. Y'all good on what we do?" Felicio turned to look at the other two.

Zora yelled out, "I'm straight with it."

"Me too." Khari nodded her head in agreement.

Felicio turned back around to face April.

"Now, I don't want to hear no more 'bout no whack ass feet fetish shit! Either get it how we getting it or move the fuck out."

It was cold, but she wanted her to get the point.

April nodded her head and sat back defeated.

She grabbed her glass and downed all the mimosa in it.

CHAPTER FOUR
CREEPY JOINT

The apartment was still and motionless.

Only Felicio and April were home. Although you wouldn't know it as they were in their own bedrooms, in their own worlds, not interacting with one another.

Zora and Khari were out tearing the malls up shopping.

April's room was cloaked in a dim, hazy twilight as the fading sun cast long shadows through the half-closed blinds.

She laid face up on her bed, she picked at the pimples on the side of her nose as her mind wandered full of thoughts and emotions. The weight of the unspoken feelings of rejection pressed heavily upon her.

Not being a person who lets shit ride, she contemplated how she could approach Felicio to talk about her emotions. Which she knew Felicio hated.

The silence was stifling, suffocating even, and April yearned to break that shit.

She had to or she felt she would explode.

She rolled onto her side, staring at the closed door that separated their rooms. The sound of muffled R&B music seeped through, a reminder of Felicio's presence just a few steps away.

April's heart pounded as she sat there trying to muster up the balls to push off. Afterall, the last time she threw caution to the wind and went for hers, she was utterly embarrassed.

Shaking the recollection out of her head, she summoned up her courage and swung her legs off the bed. Her feet met the cool hardwood floor as each press moved her closer to King's room.

She inhaled long and deep before snatching her door open.

She walked up and approached Felicio's door, pausing before she knocked to place her ear near it and listen.

When she didn't hear anything but music, she knocked.

Nothing.

She knocked again, but this time more forceful to be heard over the music Felicio had playing in the background.

Suddenly the music stopped, and Felicio yelled, "Sup?!"

That was April's queue to enter.

"Aye...um...you busy?"

"Jive, but what's up?" Felicio asked, sitting up straight on her bed.

"Yeah...I kinda wanted to talk to you." April said, looking all around the room while shifting her weight from her left to her right hip.

She was clearly nervous.

"Look, bro, just say what's on your mind, it's cool."

"Ok, what changed with us?" She asked.

Felicio sat back against her plush headboard and said, "What you mean?"

April looked down. "When I first moved in, our relationship was tight, or so I thought. We would stay up all night and talk and binge on Cartel Urban Cinema movies."

Felicio chuckled.

"But somewhere along the line we became distant." She looked up at Felicio. "Or rather you became distant from me, and I don't understand why."

Felicio took a deep breath and chose her words carefully.

"Look, bro, you my folks and we cool, nothing's changed with that. But I can't lie, you kinda threw me when you pushed up on me." She admitted. "It reminded me of how everything with us started. You know with the Catfish shit." Felicio continued.

April closed her eyes and shook her head.

She knew this may come back to bite her, but she was so eager for the chance to be near Felicio that she was willing to keep the lie alive so that they could just be cool.

When Felicio met April through the *LOP* website, it wasn't this version of herself that she showcased. Instead, it was a fem who looked nothing like April.

Felicio entertained her for a month or so and liked her instantly. But it wasn't a sexual attraction that developed, instead a friendship blossomed leaving April disappointed.

Not really what Felicio was looking for, but it was cool as the two seemed to have things in common.

However, Felicio wasn't one for the bullshit that most Catfish bammas pulled. She may give you a courtesy if a meet up in person was canceled and maybe even one canceled facetime, but niggas wouldn't get more than that.

So it came a point in time where April had to either face the music or lose the connection she built with her altogether.

And that's just what happened.

They met face to face, and Felicio was heated that April lied.

She didn't look anything like the pictures posted on her account. The woman Felicio saw was softer, prettier and easier on the eyes. She was about to throw the whole month of April away just so she wouldn't say her name again.

But April was good, she eventually convinced her that it was always her, just not her actual picture. And since their relationship was built on being friends first, and not romance, there was nothing to lose.

And then she said the magic words, "I always wanted a family. People who would take care of me, like I wanna take care of them. All I'm asking for is a second chance."

It worked!

Felicio looked upon her as a friend and they became really close, even sharing deep details about their tumultuous lives in foster care. Felicio would talk about her past, her tough upbringing and hopes for the future.

But April didn't share much about the years gone by, claiming to be no one, from nowhere.

Someone else may have picked up on the omission, but Felicio needed someone to *see her* in the hopes that she would eventually *see them*.

That's how April ended up becoming one of her roommates and everything was cool. Had she paid attention a little more, she would have seen April's long gazes at her from across the room. How when she would take a shower, and leave the door cracked, someone would open it wider.

The girl was obsessed, and her plan was solid.

To get Felicio to fall in love.

But it didn't work. Instead, all she did was overstep.

Now she had to deal with the outcome of her actions causing Felicio to push back.

"I agree, that wasn't the right time or place to do that, and I'm sorry." April said.

"Sorry not enough," Felicio replied. "I need to know right here and right now that you can accept what I'm giving you."

"What's that?" She squinted.

"A brother," Felicio said. "Like we planned."

"Can I ask you something first?"

Felicio hesitated before she answered but said, "Yeah."

"I've seen you go from woman to woman, including our roommates, so what is it about me that you can't get with? Am I not attractive?"

Felicio rolled her eyes and wiped a hand down her face. She was visibly annoyed and would rather stick pins under her toenails than to be having this conversation.

She was not a person who wanted to discuss feelings and shit.

That's one of the reasons she did so much bed hopping, because the moment a woman wanted to talk about emotions with her, she'd move onto the next.

She sat back up fully, "April, I don't know, I mean you 'aight, but you just not my type and I picked up on that online, in the beginning, even before I met you in person, you know that. So, it doesn't have anything to do with looks, just vibes I guess, I can't really explain it beyond that."

"Am I really box shaped?"

"What?"

"You called me box shaped last night."

"Oh...I was drunk. And mad." She waved the air. "Nothing more."

She looked down. "Well, is it because I'm not a Fem?" April pressed.

"Maybe, but not really...I don't know. What I will say is be easy, sometimes I feel like you real intense and that can push a nigga like me into the next galaxy. I don't do intense, from nobody, in any form."

April nodded her head as she took in her words. "Is there anything I can do? Anybody I can be? To make you see me?"

"April, I–."

"Just try me," April said standing up. "In the bedroom and–."

"Fuck is wrong with your ears! I don't want you! I can't say it no other way." She paused. "Listen, I don't wanna hurt your feelings. I swear. So please don't make me."

Gut punched.

"Ok, I get it. Thanks." She lied as she didn't get it.

"We good?" Felicio asked, trying to make sure shit was cool between them.

"Yeah, of course." April said as she walked out her room, closing the door behind her.

As Felicio's music came on again, April wanted to cry. Turning the music on so quickly made her feel like she was just another thing Felicio had to do, to get on with her day.

Now back in her own room, sitting down on her bed, she realized that she truly didn't get the rejection and now felt an awkwardness in the air.

But she also knew that she was skating on thin ice so she needed to relax and try to show Felicio that she could be chill.

She vowed to make sure that the next opportunity she had, she would be the friend that Felicio needed her to be.

Even if the shit hurt.

Zora and Khari were still out in them streets when Felicio decided to hit the shower. She had plans to go grab a few drinks at her favorite lounge and hit up pink dress since their convo didn't annoy her.

She got up and entered the bathroom from the door connected to her bedroom.

After pissing, she eased under the warm water from the head.

In the next room, April heard the water running and decided to open her door in an attempt to catch a glimpse of Felicio coming out of the shower naked.

Again.

But when she remembered that Felicio didn't have to come into the shared hallway to get into her room, she had to think of another plan.

"Let me see if she locked the door leading to the hallway." She said to herself.

She crept up to the bathroom door and gently turned the knob.

It was unlocked.

She felt her heart race as she slowly opened the door. It let out a creek that caught April off guard and she farted.

"Aye, I'm in here!" Felicio yelled out after hearing the door squeal. "Who that...who there?"

Not knowing what to do and starting to panic, April yelled out, "Oh, my bad, I didn't realize you were in here. I'll use the other bathroom."

"Oh...aight."

Felicio went back to the business of washing her ass when she had a suspicion overcome her and the hair on her body stood up.

Feeling like something was off, she pulled back the shower curtain slightly to take a peek using the bathroom mirror and what she saw gave her the creeps.

April, who she thought left out, was just standing there, staring in the direction of the shower from the hallway.

Yikes!

CHAPTER FIVE
PARTY OVER HERE

The modern apartment was full of laughter and music this evening as the roommates were in the thralls of an intimate gathering.

Zora asked Felicio to put together a small party which was not an uncommon event that they did often.

She felt like there had been some weirdness popping off in their spot and she wanted to eliminate it with some good old positive energy and fun.

The living room was transformed into a dance floor vibrating with the sounds of Moneybagg Yo's, *Quickie,* floating through the atmosphere.

Felicio, always the charismatic host, moved with an air of confidence and magnetism. This nigga always commanded the attention of the room whether she set out to or not.

"Aye...somebody bring me a plate of mumbo wings and another Strong Island!" Felicio yelled out to no one in particular.

April, who was trying to be on her best behavior after being weird the other day, once again, decided to fulfill her request.

Afterall, she wasn't doing anything anyway.

A Spades game was in action between Zora, Khari and two of Felicio's friends, Dandy and Les.

Dandy and Les were gay, funny and always brought bottles which is why they fucked with them.

So the only one that could answer the call would have to be her or Felicio's only other friend in attendance, Switch.

April jumped up from the table, "I got you."

"Bring me another Cut Water, suga." Switch yelled out.

"Fuck is wrong with your feet, *suga*?" April mocked.

"Ohhfff," Switch said with a hand to his chest. "If you don't want to get it, just say that sis."

April rolled her eyes and continued into the kitchen. She had only agreed to get Felicio's shit but wasn't about to be serving other niggas all night.

When she handed the plate and drink to Felicio, she motioned with her head for her to set it down on the bar which was near the table where the game was going down.

"What's score? Me and April got winners." She yelled out.

April smiled, excited for the opportunity to be Felicio's Spades partner, although she was also nervous.

Most people didn't just play Spades, they set out to destroy their opponents. So, if you didn't play well, you could be embarrassed which means you had to come correct.

Especially when partnering with Felicio.

She played what folks would refer to as jailhouse Spades.

Meaning if anybody sat at that table against her, it didn't matter who it was, she would purposely say whatever she could to make them mad. And whoever was her partner, she expected them to level up too or they would also be delivered.

She got it honest too. It was one of the few things she got from her father.

Knowing this, April had to come with her 'A' game or else.

"We up 300 to 200 on 'em," Dandy said. "I know they 'bout to take a blind but it ain't gonna work. We only need 5 books."

"Oh, so y'all only going to 350, huh?" Felicio asked.

"Yeah, we didn't want to completely obliterate the children."

Zora dealt the cards and yelled, "Oh, no sweetie, we getting ready to run a Boston and set y'all so don't get too comfortable at this table."

"Aw shit, this I gotta see," Felicio grabbed her plate from off the bar and walked over to the table.

She immediately opened her can of Cut Water Long Island Iced Tea and took a huge gulp.

April resumed her original seat and made sure she paid close attention to the current game.

She decided not to drink because she wanted to ensure she was sharp when she became Felicio's partner.

Shit was about to get real, real fast.

Fifteen minutes later the game was done and Dandy and his partner Les, handed Khari and Zora their asses.

They lost and lost horribly.

As they got up and made the walk of shame away from the table, April anxiously took her spot.

Excitement was an understatement to describe what she was feeling. This was an opportunity to prove she was good as a *partner*.

"Aight, Ary, let's drop these fools!" Felicio said playfully as she took her seat directly across from April at the table.

"Please, love, we getting ready to send y'all just like we sent your little roommates." Dandy retorted.

"And in your own home too." Les laughed. He grabbed all the cards to shuffle them.

"First deal bid itself, and no sandbags." Felicio yelled out to establish the rules of the game right up front.

"Baby, please, you ain't said nothing." Les started to deal out the cards. "It's go time."

Zora walked over to the bar to pour two shots of tequila and skipped the music selection that currently boomed through the speaker.

She wasn't in the mood for soft R&B now and searched instead for some Megan Thee Stallion.

When she was satisfied with the song choice, she walked the shots over to the table and placed one glass down near Felicio and the other ounces near April.

Felicio, already almost busted drunk, downed her shot before it hit the table fully. "Yes, sir! Time to move niggas out they seats."

April didn't touch her shot. She was fully concentrating on ordering her cards in her hand to put all the suits together.

For real she was too stiff.

Although she wasn't a shit talker like everyone else at the table, this wasn't just a game to her.

It was serious business.

"April, you ready, bro?" Felicio yelled out holding the lead card in her hand up near her forehead.

"Girl, throw out already!" Dandy, who couldn't take it anymore, shouted.

Everyone laughed including Felicio.

Making a choice, she dropped the first card down on the table.

The Ace of hearts.

Les dropped a heart card, followed by April who dropped a heart and finished up with Dandy who did the same.

Since no one threw out a card that was higher than Felicio's, her and April won that book.

"This how it's 'bout to be all night, girls." Felicio laughed as she teased her opponents.

"Just come on, asshole."

"Here you go," Felicio placed down the Ace of Clubs.

However, instead of the same session happening around the board this time with club cards, Les cut her card with an Eight of Spades.

"Oh you ain't in the club over there?" Felicio asked him. "Already?"

Les threw his head back and laughed.

"Yes, partner!" Dandy yelled out. "We about to bump these niggas!"

"Man that's 'aight, I know my partner got my back." Felicio said, looking across the table.

April was nervous but wasn't about to let her down. She looked through the cards in her hand and made her selection.

She threw out a Jack of Spades.

Everyone looked shocked.

"I know good and damn well that child has some clubs in her hand. I call foul." Dandy shouted. "And one bet not flow."

"Nah, my partner know what she doing." Felicio came to her rescue.

All eyes turned toward April.

She looked down at her cards where she saw four clubs.

She blinked rapidly as if she were seeing things.

She wasn't!

Them clubs had been there the whole time and she just got called out for trying it just to impress Felicio.

"Oh, damn, my, my bad, fam. I thought these were Spades." April lied.

Felicio rolled her eyes and sipped on her Long Island.

"Bitccchhhhh, you lucky we can't force a renege. But thank you for the peek." He winked. "Now, put out that club suga and let us take our book please and thank you." Les laughed.

April dropped a Seven of Clubs down and sat back in her seat.

It was only one hand, but when she glanced over at Felicio and saw the annoyance on her face, she felt defeated.

"Man, I need a new partner." Felicio yelled out upset. "Because this chick trippin'!"

Everyone cut their eyes over to April.

"Uh uh, don't do that." Les chastised Felicio. "Stop being a bully and let this child play."

Felicio was heated.

She didn't like to lose and felt that if she continued the game with April that's exactly what would happen.

By C. WASH

Before she could come up with a plan, Zora said to the room, "Did I tell y'all 'bout the club the other night?"

"No, girl, what's the tease?" Switch yelled out from his seat near the kitchen.

"So this drunk nigga got to arguing with April in the middle of the floor and you know we wasn't having it." Zora continued.

April's eyes became big as saucers. She wasn't sure about how much of that night she was gonna share but it made her nervous.

"So we rolled up, woo woo woo long story short, all of us got tossed out." Zora continued.

"Girl, that's why I don't do the gay clubs no more." Dandy explained. He threw out a card.

"Bitch, you act like the children at the straight clubs are giving anything better! They all a mess." Les chimed in.

Dandy laughed.

Felicio shook her head, irritated that the story in the club came back up but more importantly, that April was still her partner.

So she tried another tactic to get a partner switch and to chop Zora's story up.

"Fuck all that," Felicio said. "The real story is that when we came back you know how I do...me, Zora and Khari kept the party going." Felicio bragged with a huge smile on her face.

"Y'all asses is so nasty." Switch laughed. "Up in here licking and scissoring each other."

Khari smiled and Zora smirked and took a shot.

"What's the big deal about this story since you cut Zora off? I thought you were serving tea. Y'all always in here fucking." Dandy asked, sitting back in his seat.

"The deal is, April tried to slide up into the lair too. You know I don't get down with friendly fire." Felicio shook her head, having total recall of April's naked body almost sent her.

April's breath quickened and she shut her eyes tightly in embarrassment. She couldn't believe that Felicio was putting her out there in front of everybody. Public embarrassment was a fear of hers which she shared with Felicio at length.

So why was she doing this?

"Aye, young, I was pissed! I was already tight about her trying to kiss me in the club, but—"

"Wait, what?" Zora asked.

All eyes in the room popped open because no one knew about that shit.

"Yeah, slim tried to slob me down near the bar." Felicio laughed.

April wanted to crawl under the table and power drive herself into the floor she was so mortified.

But Khari shook her head as if she wasn't surprised at hearing this news.

Switch placed his hand over his mouth in shock and shook his head too.

Dandy's mouth was agape and Les tried to muffle his laughter while he looked over the top of the cards in his hand at April.

Felicio continued to chuckle. "I wasn't wit' the shits."

That did it.

"All you had to do was say get up," April said, eyes watering.

"I did. In my own way."

"I will never forget this." She threw her cards down and hit it to the bathroom.

"You's a messy bitch." Les wagged his index finger in her direction and shook his head. "But I like it."

"Switch, take her place." Felicio directed and took another sip of her drink.

IN THE BATHROOM

April slammed the bathroom door shut and pushed in the button on the knob to lock it.

Suddenly her jaws felt hot and began to fill with water and her stomach flipped.

She immediately turned toward the toilet where she threw up into the bowl.

As she stood there crouched down over the porcelain, guts emptying, she was devastated.

How could Felicio embarrass her like that in front of all them people? She couldn't comprehend what would have caused her to do that.

When she had no more to give, she flushed the toilet and rinsed her mouth in the sink. She then pulled back the shower curtain and crawled into the tub where she laid down and started to cry.

But these weren't sad or sorrowful tears, these were angry tears.

She knew that she was the new girl into the spot and that could mean a bit of a hazing period, but she was already sick, literally, of being the butt of the joke and being laughed at and not wanted.

By C. WASH

She sniffed back snot that threatened to drip down out her nose.

While she laid there and allowed her embarrassment to turn into anger, she silently pledged to never let that happen to her again.

CHAPTER SIX
THESE NIGGAS

Smoke filled the air as Felicio took a long pull from her blunt, her fingertips skillfully maneuvered the steering wheel of her sleek black Cadillac XT5.

She was lifted and in a zone as the bass-heavy beats of Gucci Mane and Kodak Black's, *King Snipe,* thumped through the speakers, enhancing the gritty atmosphere.

The city lights blurred past her as she cruised the streets, her mind focused on the mission ahead.

Light Urgent Care.

The name itself was ironic, considering the nature of her visit. But for Felicio, it was just another stop on her quest to maintain control over her kingdom.

She needed to secure the goods, the lifeblood of her operation, from the nurse who was her longtime friend and trusted supplier.

As Felicio pulled into the parking lot, her truck exuded an air of quiet authority. The dimly lit area provided a veil of secrecy, shielding the illicit transactions that occurred there under the cover of night.

Once at the location, she parked near the entrance, scanning the surroundings with sharp eyes. The tension in the air was thick, a silent acknowledgment of the risks they all took to maintain their way of life.

Chanel Whitaker, the thirty-five-year-old nurse turned plug, stood near the entrance, her fierce presence demanding attention.

Her colorful, long acrylic nails clicked against her phone as she barked instructions to her clients in the background.

She was a movement and a whole force to be reckoned with, unapologetic and unyielding.

But also beautiful and sexy as fuck.

Felicio stepped out her truck, her aura radiating confidence. She walked towards Chanel and bent down to grip her 5' 5" frame up into a big hug that lifted her off her feet.

Chanel loved being scooped up by Felicio.

"Hey, boo, them eyes real low. Why you ain't save some to hit with me?" She asked Felicio, noticing her high. "Selfish ass."

She laughed. "'Cause you at work."

"Man, fuck this job, for real." Chanel handed over a small package to her. "You know why I'm here."

"My, bitch!" Felicio said, grabbing the package and dropping it into her backpack.

With her other hand she handed Chanel a wad of cash that she tucked into her ample bosom.

"Your folks gone, right." Felicio asked, referring to Chanel's supervisors.

"Hell yeah, and I shorted out the cameras the other day and they not back up yet, we good."

"Bet! When can we meet up again for the next drop?"

"Give me about a week or so to get more in. I'll hit you when it's time." Chanel instructed.

Felicio flung the bookbag over her right shoulder and put her fist up for a pound.

Chanel met her fist bump and smiled. "You gonna stop looking at me with them eyes."

Felicio grinned. "Go 'head, young."

Just as Felicio was about to retreat to the safety of her ride, the atmosphere shifted.

The sound of sirens pierced through the air, sending a shockwave of panic through the parking lot. Within moments, the flashing lights of police cars illuminated the scene, casting an eerie glow on the chaos that was about to unfold.

In a split second, the lot transformed into a battleground.

By C. WASH

Chanel's face contorted with rage as she realized what was going on. She spat furious curses at the approaching police officers, her voice dripping with defiance as if she was in the right.

So what she was stealing them people's product.

They weren't supposed to catch her!

Fake nails, once symbols of power and allure, scattered across the pavement like sunflower seed shells.

Felicio's heart pounded in her chest as she assessed the situation.

Her mind raced, calculating her options. But before she could react, the police vehicles swiftly maneuvered to block her path, trapping her within their clutches.

She clenched her jaw, frustration bubbling within her.

The weight of the package on her back felt heavier, as if it symbolized the burdens she carried.

The officers approached, their stern expressions a testament to their power. They would slap them handcuffs on their wrists so help them God.

"Step away from the vehicle, hands where I can see them!" One of the officers commanded, his voice laced with authority and suspicion while his hand hovered over his weapon.

Felicio complied, as she slowly stepped back from her truck. She raised her arms in surrender.

When she did this, the bookbag slipped from her shoulder, falling to the ground with a muffled thud, threatening to expose their secret.

As she stood there, now handcuffed, surrounded by law enforcement, the reality of the situation sank in. The consequences of her actions loomed over her head.

Meanwhile, Chanel continued her tirade, "Y'all motherfuckas gonna be sorry if you don't get these cuffs off my beautiful black ass."

"If this your ass you in trouble, now shut the fuck up," one of the officers yelled.

Her voice rising above the commotion. Her fury echoed through the parking lot, a testament to her refusal to be silenced.

The scene was a bit much, pure chaos.

These bammas rolled up so deep you would've thought they was trying to capture Rayful Edmonds again.

Felicio's eyes met Chanel's, a silent exchange of understanding passing between them.

Something went the fuck wrong.

The only question was how?

As the officers closed in, Felicio couldn't help but feel a surge of adrenaline coursing through her veins.

She knew she had to keep her wits about her, even in the face of imminent capture. Her mind raced, searching for an escape route, a way to turn the tables on these niggas.

But there was no use.

They had them both in their grasps.

"Let's see what we have in this bag." The officer said as he bent down and retrieved Felicio's bookbag.

Sweat began to form on her forehead.

Chanel tried to get out, God bless her, but it didn't matter. "Get the fuck off me!" She continued to yell as if anyone cared to listen.

Felicio on the other hand was stuck.

The female officer walked up to Chanel and began to pat her down. Her hands glided up and down her curvaceous body.

"If you wanted to feel a bitch up, just say that sis." Chanel said to the officer.

She ignored her and went about the work of her search. When she got near her breasts, she smiled.

Chanel rolled her eyes as the officer pulled out the stack of money that had been given to her moments earlier.

"That's mine! Don't think you about to steal it either." She yelled.

The officer bagged the cash and held it up towards the other officer near Felicio.

"Well now, we got pills and cash. Looks like an exchange to me." The officer declared.

Felicio didn't say anything, and she purposely kept her face blank.

"Don't worry, you don't have to speak. In fact, you have the right to remain silent, anything you say can be used against you in..."

The officer rambled off Felicio's Miranda rights to her as her mind went blank.

She never saw this coming and because of it, she didn't have a plan of how to get out of it.

Her thoughts went to her friends in the apartment and what would happen to them if she had to do real time for this.

She was the King Dom in the castle.

Without her, how would they maneuver and survive?

As she was being placed into the back of the police cruiser, she knew she didn't have an answer for the many questions swirling around in her head.

But the one thing she did know was that she needed to get herself out of this shit now.

CHAPTER SEVEN
CHARGE UP
MONTHS LATER

Six months passed since that fucked up night in the parking lot at the urgent care, and Felicio had been engulfed in a whirlwind of emotions.

She walked out the jailhouse gates alone, her newfound freedom clashed with the heavy burden of unanswered questions and a fractured family dynamic.

The air outside tasted sweet, a major contrast to the suffocating atmosphere of her confinement. Yet, despite the relief of her release, a pang of hurt lingered deep within her.

She was fucked up because after making several attempts to contact her people, who she now considered her fake ass family, during her time behind bars, her calls had gone unanswered.

Leaving her feeling abandoned and bewildered.

Now, as she stood on the outside, she couldn't help but feel a sense of detachment.

Old scars of her past felt like they were being pushed into her present, leaving her grappling with a sense of betrayal and abandonment.

Not again.

She still didn't understand what happened or why they had turned their backs on her.

Looking around and coming out of her thoughts, she noticed a bus depot across the street from the jail.

She decided to head over there while she contemplated her next move.

Felicio sat down on a bench and dug through her personal effects in the plastic bag that the guard handed her earlier that day.

She retrieved her wallet and glanced through it to make sure all her items were there.

Next, she fished out her cell phone. She needed to see if it still worked or at the very least see if she could use it on the Wifi setting.

But just as she feared, that joint was dead.

She scanned the station to see if anyone had a charger she could borrow when she noticed a charging port near a column across the room.

She jotted straight to it and began to charge her phone.

After ten minutes, completely lost in her thoughts, Felicio was startled by the sound of her phone vibrating from the bench she sat it on.

It had been a minute since she received a call or tried to make one without asking for permission, so it was weird. And yet it also symbolized her freedom.

She retrieved her cell and held it up to her face. Her eyes widened as she saw Chanel's name flashing on the screen. It was an unexpected lifeline, a connection to the world she had left behind.

"Hey, it's Chanel," her voice crackled through the line.

"I know who it is." She squinted and looked up at the clock on the wall.

"I heard you were out, been calling you for a minute trying to catch you but your phone kept going to voicemail until now."

"Yeah, I'm out. I guess you out too, huh?"

She laughed but not seriously. "Bitch, I've been trying to find out who else got caught up in this mess, but I'm in the fucking dark."

She frowned. "You know I hate when you talk to me like that." Felicio reminded her.

"Like what?"

"Calling me bitch and—."

"After everything we went through together, you still playing soft?"

She sat back a little. "Chanel, the last thing I feel like is playing games right now."

She sighed. "Okay...I get it."

"Are you 'aight?" Felicio asked, sitting on the bench and looking out the window towards the jail that had been her temporary home.

"I'm as good as I'm gonna be." She paused. "What about you?"

"My mind fucked up. For real." She dragged a hand down her face and put her bag on the bench. "How long you been out?"

"Ten days earlier than you," She paused. "But trust, I been moving in slow motion and silence."

Felicio breathed a sigh of relief and concern. Because the way the police rolled up at that exact moment had her distrusting everybody. Even Chanel who she knew was solid.

After all, she was arrested too.

"What you know?"

"Chanel, I was kept in the dark during the whole ordeal. But I can tell you I stood tall too."

"You better had."

"Go 'head with that shit, shawty." Felicio laughed.

"Look, I got some money for you. It ain't much, but it should be enough to hold you over for a minute."

A flicker of gratitude surged through Felicio's heart.

In that instant, she realized the depth of Chanel's loyalty, her unwavering commitment to their bond. It was a powerful reminder of the connection they shared.

"I don't know what's up, but I will say don't trust nobody, Felicio."

"Not even you?"

"I said nobody. I'll meet you later for the paper."

The line fell silent for a moment, as if the weight of their unspoken words hung in the air leaving Felicio sitting there, her heart filled with more anger as she recalled the past six months.

While she had vowed to protect Chanel and the family she made, it was obvious that they didn't feel the same.

When she first got arrested, days turned into weeks, and Felicio found herself face-to-face with relentless cops.

The interrogation room was cold and lonely, but she remained solid, her walls fortified by the loyalty she felt towards her friends.

But the police had a mission and he wanted to break that shit up.

One of the cops' eyes bore into hers, full of frustration and curiosity. "Felicio, we know you a small player. We need names, details. You can protect yourself and help us take down who's backing you."

Felicio met his gaze with steely determination. "I don't know what you're talking about."

"So you trying to tell me that the pills we found in your bag that was on your back weren't yours? And that you have no idea how they got in there."

Felicio looked up at the detective and said, "I'm not trying to tell you anything."

"You realize that you going down for this no matter what you say or refuse to say, right?" The second detective dude in the room asked her.

"Yep, it's a wrap for you, what we want to know now is who else is involved in this little operation of yours?" The first detective dude asked.

"Besides nurse black and beautiful."

"Like I said, I don't know who or what you talking about." Felicio lied.

"You really gonna sit here and act like you don't know her and that we didn't just run up on y'all during an exchange?"

"Sir, I was just leaving the clinic. I don't know that lady and have no clue what y'all talking about. Can I have my lawyer?"

Felicio may have been conceited at times and a lady killer, but what she wasn't was a snitch.

She cherished the family she built and wanted to protect them at all costs.

Her lips remained sealed, her silence serving as a shield against the cop's persistent questions.

No matter how much they threatened, and they did the most, she refused to give them the satisfaction of breaking her down.

Now out and free on a technicality with charges completely dropped, she had to figure out the steps to putting her life back on track, again.

CHAPTER EIGHT
MOVED ON

Felicio sat in the backseat of an Uber, her eyes scanning the passing scenery as they made their way through the neighborhood.

The streets were alive with the vibrant energy of children playing, their laughter filling the air.

Angry as fuck, she watched them from behind the tinted windows, their carefree innocence a big ass contrast to the weight she carried within her.

As the car came to a stop in front of the apartment building she once called home, Felicio's heart quickened with anticipation mingled with trepidation.

She stepped out onto the familiar pavement, taking in the sights and smells that enveloped her. The scent of freshly cut grass blended with the scent of blooming flowers, a bittersweet reminder of the life she had left behind.

"Thanks, bro." She said as she closed the car door.

As she approached the entrance, her eyes scanned the names on the mailboxes, her name conspicuously absent.

"What the fuck?" She said dumbfounded.

A sinking feeling settled in her chest, and with each passing moment, her anxiety grew.

As she got closer to her apartment, a thin sheen of sweat appeared on her forehead and her mouth began to water.

Memories of her abandonment by her father years earlier played over in her mind and she started to feel nauseous.

She hesitated for a moment before entering the building, unsure of what awaited her inside.

She took a deep long breath.

"*Fuck is really going on?*" She thought to herself.

Walking through the hallways, more memories flooded her mind. The laughter that once echoed in these corridors had now given way to an eerie silence.

She reached the door of the apartment she had shared with her family, her hand trembling as she turned the doorknob.

It was open.

Why was the door open?

They never kept it that way.

As she entered deeper, to her dismay, the apartment stood empty, devoid of the life it once held.

No culture present, no fancy furniture, no bar, no albums, just wall to wall nothingness. They shared breakfast in that place. Parties in that place. And happiness in that place.

Her mind went into overload as she experienced Deja vu. Confusion and a sense of loss washed over Felicio.

Where had her folks gone?

Why had they moved without leaving any trace?

Was this some kind of joke?

The questions swirled in her head, but they remained elusive.

What about her gear?

Her shoes?

Her hats?

Her jewelry?

She rushed to the back and into her old room but found it also empty. Everything she loved, gone.

"They did me like this?" The jail bag dropped from her hand. She was devastated and trying her best to choke back her tears.

Just as she was about to leave the apartment, the door opened.

"Hey, you!"

Felicio turned around and recognized the familiar face of the young woman standing in the doorway from the building's front office. The woman's eyes sparkled like they always did when they saw her.

At the end of the day she looked at her like she was a snack and she wanted to fuck.

It was clear.

"So you finally home huh?" The woman said, her voice laced with intrigue. She was holding something in her hand as she closed the door behind herself.

Felicio hesitated for a moment before nodding. "They bounced. Took all my shit and...and it's fucking me up."

The woman's gaze softened, and she stepped closer. "I'm sorry about that for real."

"What you doing in here?"

"I saw you walk inside."

She squinted. "So you followed me?"

"Is that a problem?" She said licking her lips.

"Listen, shawty, I'm fresh out, like all of an hour ago. I need a shower, some clean clothes and to figure out my next move. The last thing I'm trying to do is fuck."

The smile wiped off her face. "Sorry to hear that."

Felicio picked up her bag and moved toward the door.

"Wait!"

She turned around. "What?"

"I have something for you."

"I just said I'm not gonna fuck—."

She raised the envelope, extending it towards Felicio. "Nah, that's not what I'm talking about."

Surprised, Felicio took the envelope, her fingers trembling slightly. "What's this?"

"I wasn't trying to be nosey but it's a code and some information," she explained. "One of the girls who used to stay here left it for you. She didn't say much, just that you'd find what you need there."

Felicio frowned in confusion, her mind racing. "Uh, thanks," Felicio said. "Do you know where she went?"

The woman shrugged, a mischievous smile playing on her lips. "Why you worrying about them when they—."

"Do you know where the fuck they are or nah?"

She chuckled and rolled her eyes.

"No...I don't. But I can see why they don't fuck with your mean ass. You should watch how you treat people because you never know when you may need them." She walked toward the door. "Now, you got five minutes to get the fuck out. We rented this place to someone else and they moving in today."

Before Felicio could inquire further, the woman bounced, leaving her standing there with more questions than answers.

She clutched the envelope tightly in her hand.

"I can't believe how shit has changed in six months. Where the fuck do I go from here?" She said out loud.

She looked down at the envelope again.

Opening it up, she saw an address and a code on a card.

Your things are there. Have a nice fucking life.

CHAPTER NINE
MEET ME

Felicio gripped the envelope tightly in her hands as the Uber navigated through the city streets towards the storage facility.

The anticipation of what awaited her inside intensified with every passing moment.

When the car finally came to a halt, she stepped out onto the pavement, her eyes fixed on the row of orange storage units that stretched out before her.

Taking a deep breath, Felicio made her way into the management office. The scent of fresh paint mingled with the aroma of coffee wafted through the air.

"Hello, how can I assist you today?" A friendly receptionist greeted her and said with a warm smile as she approached the counter. Her voice filled with genuine hospitality.

"Yeah, I got this code," Felicio said, holding up the contents from the envelope. "I was told there's a storage unit here in my name."

The receptionist glanced at the numbers, "What's your name?" She asked.

"Felicio King."

Her eyes scanned a list on her computer screen.

After a brief moment, she nodded and walked off. Later she returned with a key that Felicio recognized immediately.

It was to her truck.

"They...they paid my note?"

"I'm not sure who you're referring to. But I believe that's to the truck that's out front in the lot. A Cadillac something."

Felicio nodded. "Oh, ok. Um...Where is this space?"

"Oh, that's Unit 312," the receptionist said, pointing towards the rows of storage units on the outside. "It's just through that door and down a bit on your left."

"Thank you, 'preciate it." Felicio replied.

She couldn't help but wonder who had arranged this. It was obvious the way they bounced that they didn't care so why the charity?

After all she did for what she considered her family, she felt gut punched but now there was hope that someone still gave a fuck.

Entering the code to her unit, she turned the knob with a satisfying click, and the door swung open, revealing a glimpse of her past life.

This unit reflected home.

As she stepped inside, her eyes widened with nostalgia.

The walls were adorned with shelves filled with neatly arranged boxes, each labeled with her name. She opened them one by one, revealing a treasure trove of hip-hop fashion that had once been her signature style.

Clothes from renowned labels like Gucci, Versace, and Fendi spilled out onto the floor, an explosion of colors and textures that she collected over the years.

Her fingertips brushed against the smooth fabric of designer tracksuits, the sparkle of her personalized jewelry catching her eye.

"All my stuff is here, neat and safe." She said to herself.

Someone did a deed.

True.

But she was still heated if she kept it a stack.

After checking that all her things were in place, she locked the unit and left out to locate her truck.

As she approached the vehicle and ran her fingers along its sleek surface. It was a symbol of freedom, of the life she once had before it was abruptly interrupted.

She had missed the sensation of driving, the wind rushing through her locs, and the familiar hum of the engine.

But before she could fully revel in the rediscovery, her phone rang, and she answered.

"Hey, it's Chanel. Come meet me."

"When?"

"Now."

Felicio sat at the dimly lit bar next to Chanel, her mind still reeling from the encounter at the storage unit. The weight of everything she owned now in her possession was both comforting and burdensome.

Chanel, already three drinks in, sat beside her, her frustration palpable. "I can't believe this shit," she muttered, her voice laced with anger. "I lost my damn job, and now I don't know what the fuck I'm gonna do."

Felicio sympathized with Chanel's predicament, her own financial situation precarious at best.

She only had the money given to her by Chanel but that was it. And she was appreciative that Chanel was willing to foot the bill for their drinks.

Her gaze shifted to the glass in front of her, contemplating the emptiness of her pockets and the uncertainty of her own future.

"Look, sis, I feel you. Shit, I'm just as lost."

"What you mean?"

"I just came from my old spot, and nobody was there." She took a sip of her beer.

"They moved? But why?"

"I don't know but fuck it, we gotta look forward, find a way to shake back."

Chanel let out a frustrated sigh, swirling the ice in her glass. "I'm trying, Felicio. I'm fucking trying. But it's hard, you know? Shit keeps piling up, and I don't see no light at the end of the tunnel."

"Well, at least you got your dude. That's more than I can say I have."

Chanel rolled her eyes but acknowledged that having her boyfriend was a start.

Felicio nodded, her eyes scanning the room, taking in the faces of the other patrons lost in their own conversations and worries.

It was a harsh reality, and she knew firsthand the struggles that life could bring. But she refused to let it break her spirit.

She looked down at her beer and back up at Chanel.

"So...what you wanna tell me, shawty?"

"Damn! Can you just hang out with a bitch before I tell you what you wanna hear? Please!" Chanel blurted out.

"Aye, I know it sounded cold. And don't think I don't appreciate what you've done and are doing for me. But...I just...I mean...I wanna know who ruined my fucking life. None of this shit is adding up."

"And you'll find out. I promise. Just stay with me for now."

Felicio nodded her head and realized she wasn't in control of this show. She had to be patient and remain at Chanel's mercy.

So instead of pressing her out, she decided to sit back and try to enjoy the moment. After all, at least she was free.

As the night wore on, the alcohol flowed steadily, loosening their inhibitions even more, and numbing their pain, if only temporarily.

These niggas were busted. Some more than others.

"What you know about April?"

"I don't get it."

"Like what is her past?"

"To be honest, all I know is she grew up in foster care like me." She leaned closer. "Why?"

Chanel, in her fucked-up state, excused herself to the bathroom, stumbling slightly on her way.

Concern etched across Felicio's face, she felt like in the condition her friend was in, she needed to watch her back. So she got up and followed behind her into the restroom.

The stench of vomit filled the air as she found Chanel hunched over a toilet bowl, retching uncontrollably.

Bending down beside her, Felicio held back her hair, offering comfort in her time of distress.

"It's gonna be 'aight, boo," Felicio whispered, her voice filled with genuine concern. "But you gotta call it quits on the Hennessey tonight."

Chanel's watery eyes met Felicio's gaze. "Felicio, there's something you need to know." She stumbled over to the sink and cut on the cold water to rinse out her mouth.

Felicio grabbed a few paper towels and held them out towards her.

"April...April's the snitch."

The paper towels floated from her hand and into the sink.

"Wh..what you just say?" She squinted trying to understand.

"April told the cops where we were and what we were doing."

Felicio's heart skipped a beat, the weight of Chanel's words sinking deep into her soul.

April, one of her friends and part of her family, had betrayed them. The revelation pierced through the hazy fog of alcohol, bringing with it a surge of anger and betrayal.

"April?" Felicio repeated, her voice barely a whisper. "You sure 'bout this shit?"

"I asked the streets and they said she been bragging about how she brought you down. I couldn't believe it, but it's true. She sold us out, Felicio."

The truth hit different.

She trusted April, confided in her, and now that trust lay shattered. Oh she was on a mission now. A fierce desire for justice and vengeance.

"Aight, shawty, we'll deal with April, trust," Felicio said, her voice steady despite the turmoil inside her. "But right now, we need to focus on getting back on our feet."

Chanel said, "I hear you but..." She grabbed her stomach, ran back to the toilet, and threw up again.

After what she just heard, Felicio felt like she wanted to throw up too.

CHAPTER TEN
NEW KING

Their new apartment had only 30% of the flavor of their last apartment. There was no sexiness, no culture and no soul. Naw, the only thing they had in this spot was cheap furniture and each other. But it was home.

April's room was dark with only a rim light above the bed that was surrounded by a myriad of cameras carefully positioned to capture every detail.

April, Zora, and Khari lay on her large California king size bed, their feet the center of attention. The room was meant to be like Felicio's, but it came up short.

Zora's feet bore the marks of adventure, the soles black.

Filthy black, like she had walked through charred remains.

The secret behind their inky appearance lay in the crusted charcoal she had deliberately stepped in, creating a striking contrast against her skin.

Khari's feet glistened with a dark, viscous syrup that seemed to cling to every contour. The sticky substance gave them a mysterious allure, inviting intrigue and fascination.

And then there was April, donning holey white socks that added a touch of vulnerability to her long ass feet.

Each hole revealed a hint of her skin, an intentional tease to captivate the viewers.

As the cameras rolled, capturing the intricacies of their feet, April's phone suddenly buzzed, interrupting the intimate atmosphere.

She reached for it and answered, her voice full of surprise and anticipation.

"Hey, it's been a while," April said, trying to conceal her inner anger. "How did you get my number?"

"That's what you gotta say to me?"

"I...um..."

Zora and Khari looked on in interest.

"I'll be right back." She whispered.

She hopped off the bed and walked into the bathroom, closing the door carefully behind herself.

"When did you get out?" She asked in a low curious voice.

"Not too long ago." Felicio couldn't let on that she knew her so called friend had betrayed her, not yet anyway. "But look, I was calling to wrap to you."

"About what?"

"For starters why you move?"

"Wanted a better place."

"The girls with you?"

"You know they are."

"That's good. At least that way I won't have to worry about–."

"What do you want, Felicio?"

"To say I missed you. Jail made me realize a lot of things." Secrecy laced Felicio's voice. "Things I wish I said to you. So let's hook up."

"Why though?"

"What you mean why? We family, you don't miss me?"

"You know I do." April admitted not being able to control her eagerness.

"Then what's the problem?" Felicio asked seductively.

April hesitated, unsure of how much she could trust her former friend who she did wrong. But unable to resist either. After all, she wanted her from the moment she entered her life as a catfish.

"Where you wanna meet?"

"Been staying in a hotel for a few days. You can come here."

"Not first."

"Why?"

"I gotta make sure shit legit." April stated regaining control.

"You act like you can't trust me." Felicio chuckled. "And it makes me wonder why."

"Nah...I just wanna make sure everything is good first, that's all. Then I'll meet you anywhere."

"Aight."

"Cool," April replied. "There's a coffee spot by the broken-down Walmart where we used to live. Tomorrow at 4 p.m.?"

"I'll be there."

She hung up.

April's mind raced with conflicting emotions as she resumed her role in the foot-centric production.

As she performed for her client, the room buzzed with a low hum and whispered conversations. But underneath it all, April couldn't shake the unease that tingled in her veins.

The following day, as the clock struck 4 p.m., April was already at the café, a haven for people who wanted to grab coffee with a side of peace of mind throughout the day.

The scent of freshly brewed beans mingled with the clatter of plates and the hum of conversation.

She was dressed chill in a pair of skinny jeans and a form fitting hoodie with a trucker hat turned toward the back over her curly hair.

She sat at a secluded table, her gaze flitting around, searching for any sign of Felicio's arrival.

Minutes passed, and just as doubt started to creep in, Felicio walked through the café's entrance with her swag per usual. She looked good after being locked up for six months. Her locs were freshly twisted and the confidence she always possessed radiated off her as she strolled.

April's stomach flipped.

As she watched Felicio approach her table, the feelings she had before she got her locked up came flooding back, hard.

Their eyes met, an outpour of nostalgia and apprehension filling the air. Felicio arrived at the table.

"So, what's up, Ary." Felicio hit her with the personal nickname she had given her.

Pulling that one out the holster meant she came to win.

April's stomach continued to do flip flops as she masked her inner turmoil, her eyes scanning Felicio's face for any sign she knew of her deception.

The café goers bustled around them, paying no mind to the two former friends.

"I'm glad you reached out, Felicio," April finally said. "I've had time to reflect on our last encounter before you went away. And—"

"Listen, the past is the past, all I wanna do is focus on our friendship going forward. I know we lived together before, and we were good friends, but I never really got a chance to know you, intimately." She moved her chair closer to her.

Felicio was on a mission to cast her spell.

The words coming out of Felicio's mouth had her wet with anticipation.

April was in shock. This is all she wanted for the longest time. "Are you for real? All you want is to get to know me?"

Felicio leaned in closer.

"Listen, let me just cut to it, I been locked up. I haven't even been with anyone since I been home. So, I'm trying to fuck. That's why I wanted you to slide past my hotel room." She confessed.

April took a deep breath. She was completely taken aback by what Felicio revealed to her.

Felicio looked around to make sure no one was ear hustling in their business.

She reached over and placed her hand onto April's knee.

That did it!

April was so turned on now she was sure that her seat may have been wet.

"If you trying to do that too, meet me, alone. Tonight."

April's heart felt like it was skipping a beat.

She breathed heavily and decided to go for it all. "Tell me what time and where…I'll be there."

CHAPTER ELEVEN
DANCE BITCH

April stepped out of her truck, her heart pounding full of nervousness and anticipation.

Tonight was gonna be different, so she decided to embrace her femininity, stepping away from her usual tomboyish style.

Clad in a form-fitting halter top and tights, along with strappy block styled heels that her long toes hung over the top of.

She had a light beat on her face and lip gloss on her lips.

It was as if she couldn't wait to play dress up.

Doing the best she could, she went out to put on a show. She took a deep breath, trying to keep her nerves in check.

As she entered the room, she caught sight of Felicio, exuding an air of masculinity, strength, and confidence. Like a rapper on a stage ready to perform. Intricate face tattoos included.

She wanted her bad bad.

"Damn, April, you looking good, who knew you could clean up like that." Felicio complimented, a smug grin on her face.

"You think so?" She asked with a hint of self-consciousness before looking down at herself. "Really?"

Felicio's smile spread wider, grown man style as she continued to look her way. "I know so, girl."

"Good, because I feel so stupid."

"Stop it. You know you looking good over there."

She gestured for April to turn around, encouraging her to showcase her newfound confidence. But deep down, April sensed something off in Felicio's demeanor.

"What do you want from me?" April broke down and asked.

"Would I be wrong if I say everything?" Felicio looked into her eyes.

"Not if you mean it." She blushed.

Taking a moment to gather her thoughts, April mustered her courage. "Felicio, we really need to talk first," she said firmly, her voice tinged with vulnerability and determination.

Felicio's expression changed, her face contorting out of anger and bitterness.

Was she about to announce that she betrayed her? She hadn't prepared herself for her earlier confession and she didn't know if she was ready to hear it.

She wanted revenge first.

"What's up?" She clenched her jaw, the betrayal still raw within her. Despite her hurt, Felicio agreed to listen to what April had to say.

"I've spent a lot of time reflecting while you were away," April began, her voice steady. "And I've come to realize how much I hurt you with my actions. By stepping to you when you told me what it was. I mean...I never took how you would feel seriously, and I'm truly sorry."

Felicio's eyes narrowed, suspicion lingering in her gaze. "Is this a game to you, April? Are you trying to manipulate me?"

April shook her head, her voice filled with sincerity. "No, Felicio. It's all from the heart."

"So, you saying you betrayed me?"

April began to walk back her confession as she wasn't feeling the vibe Felicio was on.

"Betrayed you?"

"Yeah...betrayed me."

"Oh...no." She laughed to break the mood. "I'm saying that I was wrong for pushing myself onto you. So you don't have to do this if you don't want to."

Felicio smirked. *'I knew she ain't have the balls to confess.'* She thought.

"I don't do shit I don't want."

"But you seem angry." April stated.

Felicio had to get herself in check 'cause she had plans and she wasn't trying to let her off the hook.

"Look, let's not worry about all that right now. You know why we here, I told you what I wanted. I'm trying to fuck. What you wanna do?" She asked.

April didn't want this opportunity to slip through her fingers. "I want you." She admitted.

"Really?"

April looked deep into Felicio's eyes. "Yes, bad. More than I've ever wanted anybody or anything."

"How bad?"

April hurried up to Felicio as if she had been shot out of a cannon and when she was close enough, she went in for a kiss.

Felicio pulled her head back and said, "Naw, not yet...get on your knees."

April did as commanded.

"Take off my shoes."

April complied.

She pulled Felicio's New Balance tennis shoes off her feet and sat them neatly near the foot of the bed.

"Now what?" She asked, still sitting on her knees.

"Suck my sock."

"Wait...are you—."

"You been knew I had a kink. Now, you gonna do it or what?" Felicio whispered seductively.

She grabbed her ankles, lifted them up to her mouth and proceeded to suck the socks off her left foot and then her right.

"Now, take your tights off and dance for me. Ass in my direction." Felicio commanded with authority.

April stood up and did as told, again.

She snatched her tights down so rapidly that Felicio had to bite her lip in order to hold back her laughter.

She turned around and began to move her waist.

Her twerk job was whack but she tried, and for that the people who were on Felicio's live stream would appreciate the humor.

"Now turn back around."

When April did, she saw she was displayed on her phone. The comments were streaming down the video and the laughing emoji's were plentiful.

"What are yyyy...wh..what are you doing?" She asked, standing in front of her completely frozen.

"You know what I'm doing. You a snitch bitch! And now the world can see you a clown too." Felicio laughed.

April's heart broke as she snatched her tights off the floor and shoved her feet into them.

She had no idea how Felicio found out it was she who tipped off the police, but the truth was out.

Her stomach bubbled and she involuntarily let out a fart that was so loud it vibrated throughout the small room.

"Peeeewwwww!!!" Felicio yelled and dropped the phone out of her hand from laughing so hard.

April experienced the all too familiar feeling of embarrassment for the second time at the hands of Felicio.

She glanced over at the phone on the bed and noticed that now the crying laughing emojis rained down the live stream page wildly.

"You gonna pay for this shit! You hear me? You gonna pay!!!"

Felicio continued to laugh.

Watching her scramble from discomfort made the feeling of vengeance profound.

She was happy as fuck she pulled it off.

After finally getting herself completely dressed, April ran out of the room, leaving the door open.

CHAPTER TWELVE
SNAPPED

The air in the studio felt heavy as April, Zora, and Khari prepared for their scheduled streaming session.

It had been a few days since April's humiliating encounter with Felicio, but the sting of their interaction still lingered. She couldn't shake the hurt and confusion that settled in her heart.

As they gathered around, ready to begin their show, Khari's sickle cell flareup put her in a bad mood. She was known for her sharp tongue and quick temper when she wasn't in the mood, but this time her pain intensified her irritable nature.

Every movement seemed to cause her discomfort, and frustration seeped through her words.

"I can't fucking do this shit right now!" She spat.

"Damn, Khari, can't you do anything right?" April snapped; her words laced with bitterness. "We already booked and now your sick ass fucking shit up."

"Hold up...You aight? Because you tripping like shit!" Zora yelled.

"You know we gotta show up for the people paying. If we don't, we don't eat! I've done everything for y'all when Felicio left and I'm feeling like y'all don't really appreciate it!" April barked.

Zora took a step back so she could read April properly.

"First," she put her index finger up near April's face. "Felicio didn't leave, she got locked up while conducting business. Business that kept all of us, including you with a roof over our head and the bills paid. Not to mention that it was a fly ass roof at that, unlike where we are now." Zora looked around their current apartment.

That comment stung, April rolled her eyes.

"Second, don't act like all of us don't pull our weight. We work just as hard as you in this shit and expect you to recognize and respect that." Zora continued.

"None of that shit will matter if we out on the street because we can't pay our bills." April looked around. "And I'm sure compared to being homeless, this place is paradise." She looked over at Khari. "So get your shit together."

Khari winced at April's harsh tone and disregard of her illness. Feeling the weight of her words piercing her wounded heart.

But April had lost her mind.

The hurt from Felicio's betrayal magnified the impact of Khari's sickness. She wanted to lash out, to fight, because she was unable to reveal the real source of her pain.

Public humiliation was the devil's elixir to hear her tell it.

Khari, who needed to go and take care of herself, got up and went into her bedroom.

Zora, sensing the tension in the room, turned to April with concern etched on her face. "We need to talk."

"I thought that's what we were doing."

Zora narrowed her eyes and crossed her arms over her chest.

April sighed. "About what?"

"Bitch, where do I start?" She shot back.

"I'm not in the mood for—."

"What's been going on with you, lately? You've been distant, and something has felt off since you got that call during our live."

Hearing her bring up the word live sent her right back to Heartbreak Hotel humiliation.

"Was that Felicio that called you?" She asked.

Silence.

"Girl, was it her or not?" Zora snapped.

April's eyes flickered with sadness as she tried to find the right words. She couldn't bear the thought of revealing Felicio's streaming event or the fact that she was responsible for turning her into the cops.

Yet she yearned for the support of her friends.

"It's nothing, Z," April replied, her voice laced with a hint of weariness. "Just dealing with some personal shit. I'm good."

Zora's eyes narrowed, detecting the half-truth of it all in April's response. "Don't let your personal shit change you, April," she cautioned, her voice firm.

"The fuck is that 'sposed to mean?"

"How does it sound to you?"

April squinted her eyes and stepped closer to Zora. "Like a threat, and I don't do threats."

Zora looked her up and down. "This ain't no threat. We friends and loyalty is critical to this friendship."

"You don't think I know that shit already?" April rubbed her throbbing temples.

"Well, if you do, why would you be going off on Khari? You know she fucked up today."

Not this shit again, April thought. She was real tired of having to explain her actions. "We got clients that have paid already! I shouldn't have to keep explaining that to y'all."

"Girl, I ain't stupid. I know all that. But that's why we been saving money right? For instances like this if we can't go on."

April, being head of household now, who was responsible for all of their money, looked away.

"Uh...we are saving right?" Zora asked louder. "Because you scaring me now."

"Yes." She cut her eyes away.

"Good. So then one day off won't hurt."

"A day off today and many off soon."

Zora moved closer. "Remember what happened with Felicio? We cut her off because she tried to get us locked up for selling them pills. And now she doesn't have a family."

No, Felicio didn't try to get them locked up.

She tried to protect them.

She would never be disloyal to her friends but that was the lie April told them so that they would move out and follow her lead.

"I never want the three of us to end up like she is. Alone and looking stupid, I'm sure."

A pang of guilt shot through April's heart.

She knew Zora's words held a deeper meaning, but she couldn't bring herself to reveal the full extent of her pain. Instead, she nodded.

"I'm in charge of this family!"

Zora took a step back. "You trying to replace Felicio. Just like you trying to replace me."

"What you talking about?"

"You handle all the money and–."

"Because I put up the most to get us in here when we had to move. Remember? You ain't have no more money."

Zora looked down. "'Cause mine was tied up."

"Tied up on what?"

"Listen, I know you love living in the big bedroom, but we don't need no boss. And if we did have a boss, it would be me. Because I'm the one who pays the bills. Keep the fridge stocked and make sure we have what's needed."

"And I don't give you no money?"

"You used to…but shit been slow on your end now. And if you ask me, your funds are running low."

April's face got heated." She took a deep breath. "All I'm saying is we need order."

"No, we need you to communicate with us. That's how this family thrives. You sure you don't wanna talk about—."

April had enough.

"What I want is for you to dirty up them fucking feets and get in the bed so we can get our paper." April roared. "And since Khari's ass won't be pulling her weight, throw some syrup on them shits too. Because the new business account is in my name. Which means I rule. Can you get with that?"

Zora rolled her eyes.

"Can you or not?" April clapped her hands into Zora's face.

"Yeah." Zora walked off burnt up.

As they prepared to start the stream, April mustered all her strength, determined to set aside her personal irritation for the sake of the show. She knew she had to separate her professional duties from her little side struggles, no matter how challenging it felt, or they didn't get paid. The camera went live, and April put on a brave face and holey ass socks.

Deep down, she knew she needed time to come up with a plan to get back at Felicio.

And she would definitely get back at her.

Throughout the entire stream, April's mind wandered, replaying the moments in that hotel room.

And then suddenly she had an idea.

One that would put her on top.

April sat alone in her room, the low light casting eerie shadows on the walls. Her heart burned with a fierce determination to make Felicio pay for the pain she caused her.

Zora's words of caution echoed in her mind, a reminder of the risks and consequences that revenge could bring. But in this moment, April couldn't see beyond her own desire for retribution.

She believed that Felicio deserved to feel the same pain she inflicted.

As she scribbled notes on a crumpled piece of paper, her mind raced, concocting a plan that would make Felicio regret ever crossing her.

The bitterness fueled her imagination, painting a vivid picture of the downfall she envisioned.

"I'm sick of niggas thinking I'm soft. Thinking I'm weak. I swear, by the time I'm done with her ass, she gonna wish she never tried to play me…That's a promise!"

With that, April looked up crucial information to set her plan into motion.

CHAPTER THIRTEEN
DOM OUT

Felicio found herself caught in a bind; her living situation unraveled like a frayed weave. She couldn't keep staying in motels because they cost too much money and she needed all the ends she could get to try and get another place.

She had been crashing at Chanel's crib for the past few days, finding solace in their tight bond.

But now, her nigga had thrown down the gauntlet, claiming he couldn't 'have a dom lady like Felicio living up in his crib with his woman'.

"Girl, you gotta get the fuck up," Chanel said shaking Felicio's arm back and forth.

It was the middle of the night and Felicio had been sound asleep on the sofa when she was awakened abruptly.

"You know I hate when you talk to me like that." She said, turning over and rubbing her eyes.

"Get up." She looked back at her bedroom and then back at Felicio. "Hurry up, please. Before he come out here."

"What's wrong?" She rubbed her eyes.

"My nigga think we fucking! You gotta go."

"Fucking? Come on man, why would he think that?" Felicio asked. She wiped a hand down her face. "Let me go talk to him so–."

"No...just get up. Please. Because we can't both be out on the streets."

Now sitting upright on the couch Felicio said, "But I thought this was your spot, if your name on the lease how can he kick you out?"

"Easy! Now come on." She explained gathering up Felicio's things from around the living room. "I'll help you find a place of your own but for now you gotta dip."

"This wild." She grabbed her shit and moved toward the door.

"But don't worry, I'm gonna be with you all the way. I promise you that shit." She hugged her and shoved her closer to the door.

"I hear you."

With no other choice, Felicio left her friend's apartment and slept in her truck for the rest of the night. It was hard because she couldn't get comfortable.

She was tall.

Basketball player tall, so she needed room.

Chanel, always ride or die, felt terrible for having to put Felicio out. So, she made it her mission to find her a spot—a place where she could reclaim her independence.

A few days later, with Chanel at her side, they hit the streets, hustling through the urban wasteland of real estate. The scent of the concrete jungle mingled with the aroma of sizzling street grub, teased their nostrils as they bounced from one potential spot to the next.

Each building they stepped into held its own story, secrets waiting to be uncovered.

After a grip of viewings and some letdowns, they stumbled upon a hidden gem, tucked away in a quiet corner of the city.

The spot looked like it had been waiting for them, with its brick walls giving that upscale flair for the low.

They stepped inside, and anticipation hung in the air like a thick fog. The apartment didn't disappoint. It unveiled itself like a VIP experience, showcasing a space with endless possibilities. This was a look and with the money she had she could pay a few months out.

Big windows, that sunlight streamed through and polished wood floors.

It had a lived-in feel and clearly needed work, but Felicio was up for the challenge.

After all, it would beat living in her storage unit, which is where she had been staying.

"Man, it ain't my old spot, but shit with some elbow grease I see the potential in this joint being better." Felicio's eyes danced as she continued to take in the space.

"See, friend...That's what I'm talking about! We can do so much here. I think we found your new home." Chanel's voice oozed with confidence as she painted a picture of the life Felicio could build in this new place.

"I can already imagine the kitchen always smelling like fresh-brewed coffee. And making late-night munchie runs. Yeah, this it!" Felicio said, nodding her head in approval.

With each passing moment, Felicio's worries faded away like smoke dissipating in the breeze.

Chanel was true to her word.

Her unwavering support filled her with gratitude, reminding her of the power of true homies.

They were creating more than a crib for Felicio—they were forging a bond that would stand strong, a foundation of loyalty and love.

"Let me sign the lease before somebody take this joint, young!"

Together, they navigated the procedural maze, filling out paperwork and handling the hustle to secure Felicio's new digs.

Now, the lease had been signed, and the deposit was paid, it was a done deal.

As they stepped out of the building, a sense of accomplishment swirled around them, blending with the fresh city air and the distant sounds of urban life.

Felicio was coming to realize that with Chanel riding shotgun until she got on her feet, she knew she could conquer any obstacle, and flip the script on the narratives that had held her down for too long.

Chanel asked, "What you gonna do now? I gotta get back to Casey's mean ass for he trip."

"Going to get some furniture. Gotta sell some of my tennis shoes and buy some pieces." She sighed.

"I'll be back to help you move in." She touched her arm and Felicio was reminded of the time they were almost a thing before Felicio decided they would be better as friends.

She winked and gripped her up in a tight hug. "Thank you, shawty. I couldn't have done any of this without you." She whispered into her ear and held onto her for what seemed like forever.

Neither of them wanting to break their embrace.

It was time to do something rough to ease her future.

Felicio stood in front of the dusty steel door of her storage unit, the code clutched tightly in her hand. She took a deep breath, preparing herself for the emotional rollercoaster that awaited her inside.

The space held fragments of her past—memories carefully boxed away, waiting to be revisited.

As she lifted the door open, the scent of aged cardboard and a hint of nostalgia wafted through the air. The room was filled to the brim with crates and containers, each holding a piece of her former life.

She scanned the area, her eyes landing on stacks of shoeboxes—the treasures she had amassed over the years.

With a heavy ass heart, Felicio approached them.

One by one, she opened the shoeboxes, revealing a collection of kicks that once held a special place in her heart.

Shit, a lot of 'em still did.

Memories flooded back—each pair told a story, marking moments of triumph, resilience, and style.

But now, she had to make a sacrifice.

Felicio hung her head.

She knew she couldn't carry the weight of her past on her journey towards a brighter future.

So she became hopeful.

"Shit, it ain't like once I'm back up I can't get a whole new wardrobe." She reassured herself.

With that, a newfound boost of energy and confidence entered her spirit as she carried out the unimaginable.

Carefully she selected a few prized pairs of sneakers, ones that held sentimental value and in excellent condition that could fetch a good price.

With a few select pairs in mind, Felicio packed them up and made her way to a retail shop known for its reselling market.

The atmosphere buzzed with sneakerheads haggling over limited-edition releases and sniffing the shoes they wished to cop.

The scent of fresh rubber soles mingled with the excitement of potential deals.

She took her treasured shoes over to the counter to begin negotiations. All the while hoping they wouldn't try and dick her around.

"I can give you about $120.00 for 'em." The young white boy behind the counter told Felicio holding the neon green shoe in his hand.

"Cap!" She shouted. "A buck twenty? My man, you know these Grinches right? Kobe not even here no more. I can get way more money if I sell 'em online!" She was insulted.

"Yeah, I'm aware of what they are, but people come to us that want cash now." He explained. "If you had time to take pictures of them and upload them online and then wait for them to hopefully sell, against all the other sellers out there, you would've done that first."

Felicio sighed.

The bamma was telling the truth and she knew it.

"Aight, but $120? Come on, fam you gotta be able to do better than that. You know y'all gonna make a grip re-selling 'em to somebody else. Look at 'em, they barely worn." Felicio pleaded holding up the other shoe for closer examination.

White boy stroked his long orange colored goatee.

"Alright, $220, but that's as high as I can go."

Felicio shook her head.

"You killing me...But I'll take it. I got about three more pair too." She bent down into her bag and pulled out the additional boxes.

As she continued to negotiate with the shop owner, she couldn't help but feel a pang of sorrow.

Each transaction felt like a little piece of her identity was slipping away. Yet, with every dollar she received, a glimmer of hope sparked within her.

The cash represented the means to start anew, to create a home where she could reclaim her independence.

Once the deals were done, Felicio counted the money in her hands—a modest sum, but it held the power to transform her surroundings.

She walked out the store with empty bags and her head held high.

She pulled up on a furniture store and walked inside, her footsteps echoing against the showroom's polished floors.

She browsed through the array of couches and beds that she could afford, carefully selecting pieces that would become the foundation of her new space.

After finding what she came for and making the purchases, she realized she hadn't really eaten shit since she fucked up April's mind publicly in that hotel.

She was too focused on her mission but now her stomach told her it was time.

Belly growling, Felicio grabbed a small box of shrimp fried rice from a nearby takeout joint.

She settled down in her storage unit, at her makeshift dining area, and savored each flavorful bite. The solitude gave her a moment of reflection, allowing her to embrace the journey she had undertaken.

As she polished off the last morsel of rice, Felicio's thoughts shifted to the future.

"Come tomorrow, I get to take back my shit, my life. No looking behind."

Her gratitude swelled within her, and she couldn't wait for the morning to come.

With a smile playing on her lips, Felicio closed her eyes, envisioning the walls of her new home, waiting to be adorned with memories yet to be made.

She only hoped nothing would fuck it up.

CHAPTER FOURTEEN
SPIKED FOR FILTH

Chanel's black Mercedes Benz cruised along the city streets, so clean that everything she passed reflected off its exterior.

Inside the luxurious vehicle, Chanel leaned over and handed Felicio a steaming cup of spiked coffee after just picking her up from the storage unit.

The aroma of roasted beans mingled with the not-so-subtle hint of liquor she added, created an intoxicating blend.

She took a large sip. "Young, did you spike this shit?" She asked, popping the lid and taking a sniff. "'Cause this shit good as fuck."

Chanel winked. "What you think? It's a celebration, niggaaaaaaaa!"

Felicio took a larger grateful sip, feeling the warmth of the beverage spread through her body.

She leaned back into the plush leather seat, taking in the urban landscape passing by. The city buzzed with energy, a symphony of car horns, distant sirens, and laughter echoing through the day.

Chanel, with her confidence radiating from every pore, turned her attention to Felicio, a mischievous glint in her eyes. "So, have you spoken to April since the last time you saw her? That girl's been heavy on my mind lately."

Felicio's eyebrows furrowed slightly as she pondered Chanel's question.

She took another sip of the coffee, letting the liquid fuel her thoughts. "Naw."

"Oh, that's all you giving?" Chanel asked glancing over to look at Felicio before training her eyes back on the road.

"Haven't reached out. And ain't shit to talk about. She a rat."

Chanel nodded; her glitter laced manicured fingertips tapped on the steering wheel to the rhythm of Chris Brown's *'Under The Influence'* that played softly in the background. "I get it, boo. The struggle is real but at least she out your fuckin' life."

Felicio sighed; her gaze fixated on the passing cars whizzing by. "After all that went down, I gotta be on my own shit."

Chanel's smile widened as she nodded approvingly. "I got something I wanna tell you. About her past."

Felicio squinted. "What?"

"Did you know she was Amish?"

"Listen, I'm not trying to hear no wild ass–."

"For real. Her father was a white boy out of Mechanicsville Maryland. He fell in love with a black woman and–."

"Amish don't fuck with blacks."

"Well this one did. She worked at the same market he sold his produce at. And the community shunned him because–."

"Aye, yo, Chanel, all niggas got stories. So if you want me to feel sorry for–."

"I never said that."

Chanel nodded. "You right. But whatever you wanna know–."

"I don't wanna know shit about–."

"Whatever you wanna know," Chanel said louder. "I'll tell you when you ready. For now we can't let none of them bitches define you. This new apartment gonna put you back up. And I got another connection for pills too. So we 'bout to be real good!"

Felicio nodded and raised her cup in the air to toast to what Chanel just told her.

"Damn, how much you put in this coffee? Got a nigga feeling real saucy over here."

Chanel laughed, "Good! Vibe with that shit. Sit back and let me take care of you." She winked. "That's what friends are for."

As the Benz smoothly turned a corner, the chatter of the city morphed into the rumble of the urban landscape.

Felicio couldn't help but feel a sense of excitement bubbling up within her. She envisioned this day, and it was finally here.

The happiness she experienced made it hard to sit still in that car seat. She couldn't wait to get to her new home and just take it all in.

"So, tell me," Chanel asked, her curiosity piqued. "You fucking with anybody yet?"

Felicio sat up and craned her neck toward her, "Fucking with anybody?" She chuckled. "Shawty, I just got out and don't even have a home. What I'ma do, bring her to my storage unit to fuck on my air mattress?"

Chanel shouted. "Shit, some of these donkeys out here done fucked on and in worse."

The two friends shared a belly laugh, their voices blending with the beat of the music playing in the background.

With each passing mile, Felicio's excitement grew more intense. She felt her stomach continue to flip with anticipation.

Or maybe it was that liquor she was drinking without eating that had her feeling the fuck crazy.

A home of her own.

Sweet.

As the Benz pulled up to her new apartment building, Felicio couldn't help but smile. The delivery truck was waiting out front, ready to drop off her new couch.

She sipped the last portion of her special brew and said, "Let's do it!"

Felicio and Chanel struggled to maneuver the couch she purchased through the narrow corridors and into her new apartment's living room.

"Nigga, you need you some Dom friends that can help you with this kinda shit! I ain't built for all this." Chanel yelled barely able to hold her end up trying desperately not to break off all her nails.

"Shawty...You know them bammas was tripping! I wasn't 'bout to pay them no hundred dollars more to bring it up here." Felicio yelled out. "They was trying to hustle me. Who the fuck deliver furniture but don't deliver it inside?"

Beads of sweat formed on their brows, as they continued to move the couch in. Finally, they managed to position it in its rightful place, admiring the way it transformed the room already despite being empty.

But their moment of triumph was interrupted by a knock on the door. Felicio exchanged a puzzled glance with Chanel.

"You expecting somebody already?" Chanel whispered to Felicio while flopping onto the couch in exhaustion.

"Naw." Felicio shook her head and shrugged her shoulders.

She went to see who it was.

Standing in the doorway was the building's management, a stern expression etched upon her face.

"Hey, Mrs. Hester, is everything okay?" Felicio asked, her voice full of concern.

The apartment manager cleared her throat, her gaze shifting uncomfortably. "I'm sorry to inform you, but there's been a misunderstanding. After conducting our background check, we discovered that your criminal record is still pending."

'*Fuck*'. Felicio thought.

Her heart sank, disbelief and frustration intertwining within her. She had thought that her legal troubles were behind her. But the weight of the past came crashing down upon her, threatening to shatter all the dreams she had of a fresh start.

"Naw, the charges were dropped," Felicio insisted, her voice trembling with anger and desperation. "I can contact whoever I need to and get this straightened out." She informed.

The manager sighed, her eyes conveying sympathy and empathy. "I understand your frustration, but until we receive official confirmation that your record is clear, I'm afraid we cannot proceed with your tenancy."

"Ok, I'm not sure how long it'll take for me to get you the confirmation, but can you hold the apartment for a day or so? It shouldn't take that long. Please, just give me the chance." Felicio pleaded, her eyes full of hope. "I'm living out my car."

She shook her head. "I'm sorry, I won't be able to. We have a waiting list of people so the apartment will have to go to one of them."

Felicio's shoulders slumped, the weight of disappointment settling upon her. She exchanged a glance with Chanel, their shared sadness mirroring in each other's eyes.

"But it was all good when I filled out the application. Y'all said I was good. What changed...I mean...how—." Felicio was stuck and confused and needed answers.

"Are you trying to ask me if anyone told us about this?"

Felicio folded her arms over her chest picking up on the subtle hint she dropped. "Yeah."

She grinned as if she caught her red-handed. "Does it matter? Please take this couch along with anything else you have moved in and leave the property. I'm sorry." Mrs. Hester walked away from the door and down the steps.

Felicio was devastated.

With a heavy heart, her and Chanel made their way back down the stairs, the weight of the couch feeling heavier than ever.

As they reached the bottom, their eyes met an unexpected sight—April was sitting in a car, her laughter filling the air.

Confusion and betrayal washed over Felicio.

"What the fuck is she doing here?" Felicio muttered her voice laced with anger and frustration.

Chanel shook her head, "Oh that bitch thinks this real funny! Shit, after snitching I ain't know that she could go any lower."

Felicio clenched her fists, anger simmering within her. And then she remembered all the heartfelt moments they shared. How she shared with April her fear of being homeless again.

A fear so strong it had her choosing a life of crime just to make enough money to withstand hard times.

This wasn't just a jab.

The act April pulled was meant to keep her down low. On the streets. With no help.

"Bro, I swear to God, I'm gonna see that she pays behind this move!"

Chanel glanced over at her friend before focusing back on the road. She was scared but couldn't say she blamed her.

As the car drove away, Felicio made sure she stayed present and felt every moment of this anger so that she could use it for her revenge.

No matter the cost.

CHAPTER FIFTEEN
DRUNK THOUGHTS

Felicio sat in the barely lit storage unit in a haze, her mind clouded with frustration and disappointment.

This couldn't be home.

It just couldn't!

The taste of bitterness mingled with the burn of vodka as she took another swig from the bottle. Each sip seemed to fuel the fire within her, intensifying her anger at the recent turn of events.

She had been so close to starting fresh with creating a home for herself. But April's interference had shattered those dreams.

How could someone she called family once stoop so fucking low?

Felicio's mind churned with questions, her heart heavy with the weight of betrayal.

Seeking solace, Felicio reached for her phone and dialed Chanel's number. Her voice trembled with anger as she recounted the situation, her words laced with frustration and disappointment and the only person she wanted to talk to was her friend.

Now she knew why Casey didn't want her nowhere near Chanel.

The two were close.

As close, if not more, as she once was to Zora.

"How could she do this to me, Chanel?" Felicio's voice cracked with emotion.

"Firstly, you ain't innocent. You put her on live stream dancing and licking dirty socks?"

Felicio sucked her teeth and rolled her eyes realizing she may have gone too far out of anger. "I'm talking 'bout before all this shit. Like why the fuck she snitch? She started all this, I was just getting even behind that. Then she get me thrown out my new spot!?" Her words slurred slightly.

Chanel's voice came through the phone, heavy with concern. "I know it hurts, babe, but we'll get through this. We'll find a way to overcome every obstacle."

"Fuck that!" Felicio yelled out. "I ain't do shit to her but try and take her in and under my wing. With the stuff I know on her I could have—"

"Everybody has a reason for the shit they do. Whether you know their reason or not."

"But that's just it, I can't even imagine what reason she would have to go that hard."

Chanel let out a yelp, "I can, it's because you didn't fuck her, ain't it?"

"Man, hell naw! That can't be it, she been knew I wasn't going there with her. We even talked about it, kind of, and I felt like she understood."

"Clearly, she didn't, otherwise she wouldn't have showed up at that hotel ready to be dicked down."

Felicio took another swig from her bottle. It was true. She knew her power over April, and she aimed it right at her heart, blasting it apart.

"Listen, I know you in there getting saucy and that's cool. You get the night after the disappointing day you had. But stay focused, nigga. We need to find another place so you can get out of there. That and only that is the goal."

Felicio took a deep breath, her anger slowly subsiding as Chanel's words began to soothe her wounded spirit.

"You right, thanks for that shit. You know how much I 'preciate your ass, man."

"You know it. Now, get off my phone and get some sleep before my nigga wake up and kill us both. We gonna figure this out tomorrow." Chanel told her.

"Fuck him."

"You gonna say it to his face," she giggled softly.

"Yeah...where he at."

"Felicio stop...it's like you using your weapon against me now."

She sighed. "I'm just playing. I do like talking to you but let me stop. It's wrong. I don't wanna fuck up your shit 'cause mine in the dumps."

"You gonna be good." Chanel laughed as she looked behind her.

"How you know?"

"Because I'm holding your hand. And I'm not letting go."

"You see, that's why I call you." She sighed. "Night, friend."

"Good night."

Felicio nestled herself into her makeshift bed within the storage unit, the exhaustion of the day slowly taking hold.

She tried to drift into a fitful sleep as the darkness enveloped her troubled mind.

But just as her slumber began to claim her, she felt a prickling sensation against her sock. Stirring in her half-conscious state, she brushed it off with her other foot, dismissing it as a figment of her imagination.

But the annoyance persisted, growing more insistent with each moment.

With a sudden jolt, Felicio bolted upright, her eyes widening in horror. A gigantic rat scurried across her foot, its presence a cruel reminder of her current situation.

"What the fuck! Hell no!!" She screamed out in horror.

Panic consumed her as she fumbled for the unit's door, anxiously trying to escape the confined space and let in more light.

Her hands met resistance, the darkness obscuring her vision. Frantic and desperate, she struggled to find the latch, her heart pounding in her chest.

Finally, the door creaked up, releasing Felicio from her prison. Gasping for air, she stumbled out into the open, her anger bubbling to the surface.

Her yells echoed in the darkness, a raw expression of her frustration, betrayal, and determination.

With each shout, Felicio expelled the pent-up emotions that threatened to consume her.

The rat shit took her back.

Back to when she lived with her aunt for three days.

Back to her teenage years and the terrible memories of living in the alley near a church.

After her father abandoned her for displaying signs of being a lesbian, she wandered around the city, begging and sleeping where she could.

It was on the fucked up streets she called home where she had to fight off rats to try and rest and stay warm, night after night. The pain she felt and the things she endured she wouldn't wish on anyone.

She ended up finding herself at a church in Northwest, DC. It was located on 10th & G Streets and in their basement, they served hot food daily to the homeless in the city.

She couldn't even recall how she ended up there, but after showing up every day to eat, one of the volunteers noticed she was too young to be alone and called social services.

From that point on, she was placed into foster care where she remained until she aged out. The recollection made her even more infuriated then she had been previously.

And in that moment, she knew what she had to do.

If only to prove to herself and the world that she was a force to be reckoned with.

She called Chanel back.

"Chanel, I'm sick of this shit!"

"What happened? Why you...why you screaming?" Chanel asked, concern evident in her voice. "I thought you were going to sleep."

"I've had enough of April's games," Felicio replied, breathing heavily. She decided not to share that Mickey tried to nibble on her toes. "She thinks she can betray me and get away with it? But I got a plan, a way to bring down her whole world."

Chanel's surprise was palpable. "Wait what? Bring down her world? What you talking about?"

Felicio's determination shone through as she spoke. "I know the key to hitting her where it hurts the most—her money and her closest friend."

"Hold up, you talking about Zora ain't you?"

"Fuck you think?"

Chanel, cautious yet caring, responded, "Felicio if you do this, it's gonna make it worse. Plus, it's gonna pull people into this mess that ain't even involved. This not the way, trust me." She warned.

"So you want me to let her hit hard and do nothing? What happens when I find another spot and she sabotages that one too? I can't keep living like this!" She yelled.

"All I'm saying is fucking with a nigga's money is serious. It'll only create more pain and chaos. Like where will this end? Let me tell you about her story so—"

"This is more than revenge," she interrupted. "It's about showing her that she can't do what she want to folks with no repercussions." Felicio continued. "She struck first by having me locked up, I ain't do shit to that lady!"

Sighing, Chanel tried to reason, "Look, I understand you're hurt and angry but—"

Felicio's defiance was unwavering. "Shawty, you've always been there for me, and I appreciate you even answering the call. But this is something I gotta do. You with me or not?"

Concern etched in her voice, Chanel softly replied, "Felicio, I don't want to see—"

Determined, Felicio asserted, "I made up my mind. I'm not asking for your permission or approval. I'm telling you what I'm gonna do."

Resigned, Chanel said, "Aight, Felicio. If this is what you truly believe you gotta do, then I'ma ride with you. Just promise me that you won't lose sight of who you are in the process."

Grateful, Felicio said, "Good because I'm 'bout to ruin this bitch life."

After getting off the phone with Chanel the second time, Felicio refused to sleep in the storage unit.

She packed her a spinnanight bookbag and left.

She ended up at a lesbian bar in Northwest with one goal in mind. Find somebody fuckable and go home wit' 'em.

Now, she's done this plenty of times, but this was the first time in a long time where she was doing it because she didn't have anywhere else to go. The rat and more like them took over her home.

As she nursed her beer while sitting at the bar, she surveyed the establishment. There wasn't a whole lot to choose from but since she wasn't trying to marry a bitch, she knew she just needed doable.

When she felt herself looking too desperate, she decided to pull back and act like she wasn't looking for shit.

She smiled, because she realized that her plan worked perfectly when a cute joint came and sat right next to her.

"Hey," Cutie said, swirling the straw around in her drink.

"Sup."

They both sat in silence sipping and bopping to the music.

Felicio decided to take control because she didn't want to miss an opportunity waiting for Cutie to make a move. Afterall, she did initiate shit by sitting next to her.

"You like Kehlani's music too, huh?" She asked, kicking the convo off.

"Mmmm Hmmmm, and she fine, too." Cutie laughed.

Felicio chuckled. "She aight, not really my type though."

"Oh, yeah, what's your type?"

"Mmmm...'bout 5' 5", light brownskin, pretty eyes and dimples." Felicio described Cutie back to herself.

She giggled, "That was cute, I'll give you that."

"I'm playing, shawty. What you drinking, can I get you another?" Felicio asked.

"Oh it was a margarita, but I'm good, actually about to head home."

Felicio realized she had to speed this up or babygirl might walk out the door without her. "Damn, my bad wished I would have seen you earlier, but maybe another time. You be in here a lot?"

"Sometimes, but not too often." She replied.

"Just my luck, but I guess if it's meant for us to see each other again we will." She was gambling by rounding Cutie up, but she couldn't give off creep hobosexual vibes.

Cutie looked Felicio up and down and said, "Maybe I'll have one more."

Felicio smiled and thought, 'Got her.'

Thirty minutes later they were back at Cutie's house in her bedroom and deep into their fuck session.

Felicio had Cutie up against a wall, standing with one leg propped up on the bed as she dug her tongue in and out of her.

Her pussy dripped out onto Felicio's nose as she licked her ferociously. She was so fuckstrated that she took it out on shawty.

"Ugghhhhh...Felicio, please...Please slow down or I'ma buss all in your mouth, and I don't want to yet."

Felicio ignored her pleas and continued to lick her down. As cutie's leg started to shake, Felicio ran her tongue up to her asshole. She licked it soft and gentle until she made her way back down to her awaiting pussy and when she did, she concentrated on her clit. She sucked it sternly with her lips and tongue, stopping every so often to lick her opening.

When she noticed that Cutie's body tensed up, she went in for the kill. She covered her entire pussy with her mouth and using her tongue, she licked one last time before sucking on her clit and all her cum out.

"Oh my, God, Felicio!! Fuckkkkkkkkkkkkkk." She yelled out.

Now, it was time to get hers. Already wearing her joint, she entered Cutie from behind and began to whine her hips.

"Mmmmm....Mmmmmmm, fuck this pussy," Cutie said as she matched Felicio stroke for stroke.

She held onto her soft waist and used it to glide in and out of her. She closed her eyes and got lost in the intense feeling of being with a woman. Afterall, this was her first cheeks since she'd been released.

Before tonight, she had gotten with one broad while locked up, but it wasn't very eventful given the circumstances.

As she felt Cutie begin to speed up the whining of her waist, indicating her second nut was approaching, she pumped harder.

"That's right, sexy, throw that ass back." She encouraged, before smacking her plump ass cheek.

"Oh, fuck...I'm about to cum again," Cutie yelled out. Felicio continued to grind into her, holding her waist with her left hand as she reached her right hand around and found her clit using her middle finger.

"OOooohhhhh...OooooooHHH...Oohhhhh....Mm mmmmmmmmmm." Cutie yelled out satisfied.

"Don't move, baby," Felicio instructed as she sought after her orgasm too.

She moved her hips methodically giving into the sensation of the explosion that was ramping up within her. And a few strokes later, Felicio came hard.

As she climbed out of Cutie and layed down to catch her breath, she thought about putting the new plan into play to get back at April.

"That was nice, Cutie said curling up under Felicio's arm."

"Yeah, it was pretty nice, wasn't it?"

"You can stay if you want, you don't have to leave." Cutie told Felicio.

Normally, she would have already been up and getting dressed, but since she had nowhere to rush off too, she relaxed and rubbed Cutie's arm.

Thoughts of revenge danced around in her head as they drifted off to sleep.

CHAPTER SIXTEEN
BAMMA NIGGA

They were pushing their luck because Chanel and Felicio were in her apartment.

Chanel sat at her dining table; a plate of sandwiches neatly arranged in front of her. She glanced at her laptop, where a Zoom call was set up with her work, the camera turned off. It was her way of feigning attentiveness while she engaged in a heart-to-heart conversation with Felicio.

She was able to get a job with a medical insurance company in customer service where she worked from home.

Felicio leaned back in her chair, taking a bite of her sandwich before continuing, "I wonder how long that bitch been giving snake."

"Would it matter?"

"Naw...not really, since you never can truly know a person, only whatever they want you to know."

Chanel nodded, her eyes darting between Felicio and the laptop screen. "Yeah, it's hard to comprehend how someone you thought you knew could change like that. Where you meet her again, I can't remember?"

Felicio sighed, setting her sandwich down. "I met April online, on *LOP*. She had pictures up that made her look completely different. I mean, she lied about her whole entire appearance."

Chanel's eyebrows furrowed, her curiosity piqued. "Wait, she lied about how she looked on her profile?"

"Yeah, shawty...Ain't that what I said?"

"Well that's your first fuckin' sign there." Chanel checked her laptop to make sure she wasn't missing anything.

Felicio nodded, frustration evident in her voice. "I know, man, I know. She deceived me from the very beginning. And I dismissed it 'cause we got cool. I should've just walked the fuck out when she came in and she wasn't who she said she was."

Chanel picked at her sandwich, her mind racing. "She ever give you any other signs, besides that...Before the snitching?"

Felicio leaned forward, her expression intense. Thinking back on the beginning of her and April's friendship.

She thought about all the times she tried to push up on her and when she caught her staring and being a creep.

"Yeah, the signs were there, but I ignored them and just kept it moving not wanting to deal with it."

"But why?"

Silence.

"Why though?"

Felicio took a deep breath. "I don't know anymore. I guess I..."

"Liked the attention," Chanel said, finishing her sentence.

"That's not it."

"You sure?"

Felicio waved the air. "Anyway, I've been thinking about my plan. I need Zora away from her. I wanna see if she's managing their money and if she is, I want her gone."

"And you think Zora will leave with you?"

"I don't know. But I wanna try."

Chanel's eyes widened with concern. "Felicio, I get that you're hurt, for real, but be careful how you go at April."

Felicio took a deep breath, her voice filled with resolve. "She should've thought about how she came at me."

"So you serious?"

"No mercy."

Chanel reached across the table, placing her hand gently on Felicio's. "Just promise me that you'll prioritize how far you'll take it. Like I said a few days ago, we got money to make."

Felicio winked. "Just get me that number from your peoples at the cell phone company. I'll handle shit from there."

The two friends sat at the table in silence, munching on their food as Chanel continued to fake work.

Suddenly, the front door swung open, and in walked Chanel's boyfriend, Casey.

Casey's face twisted into a scowl as he laid eyes on Felicio. "Hold up! What the fuck is this joint doing in here again, Chanel?" He barked, his voice filled with anger and suspicion.

Felicio, feeling the tension rise in the room, tried to calm the situation down.

"I ain't mean to cause no trouble, champ. I was just having lunch with Chanel," she replied, her voice steady but defensive.

"*Just having lunch with Chanel?*" Casey crossed his arms over his chest, his eyes fixed on Felicio. "You think I don't know what you after? You been trying to get with my bitch since day one!"

Chanel rushed to intervene, stepping between Casey and Felicio. "Enough, Casey! Stop jumping to conclusions. Felicio is my friend, and that's it."

Casey's glare intensified; his nostrils flared. "Naw, I ain't buying that shit, Chanel. I can see what's going on. I know she's trying to slide in between us and it ain't happening."

Felicio's frustration grew, her voice rising as she defended herself. "That's not true, Bro! I would never do that to Chanel. I promise, we just friends, and I respect her relationship with you, fam."

"I ain't your bro or your fam! And you can keep your fuckin' promises." Casey said, moving closer towards Felicio.

The air was becoming thick and if Chanel or somebody didn't do something, shit was gonna get crazy, fast.

Since this was his house and she knew how he felt about her, Felicio decided it was best to remove herself from the situation.

"I'ma dip, it's cool. No worries." She grabbed her stuff and walked out the door, closing it behind herself, mad as a bitch.

Chanel came darting out after her. "Felicio!"

She turned around. "What?"

"I'm sorry about that shit."

"Why would you have me in that bitch when you knew he'd be coming home?"

"I ain't stupid. I didn't know he was coming. He popped up."

"Look, I ain't trying to be dealing with all this added drama. From now on we meet up outside, that way—."

Chanel looked down.

Her face full of sorrow. "We can't be friends no more."

"What?" Felicio asked in shock and moved closer. "What you saying?"

She shook her head. "I'm sorry."

Felicio squinted. "Hold up, you letting that fool come between us?" She pointed at the building.

Chanel closed her eyes and sighed. "He made threats that he's been known for backing up. And I don't want him to do anything to you."

"Shawty, I can't even believe this shit." Felicio said feeling like her world was crashing down around her.

"I'm sooo sorry." Chanel's eyes began to water.

Felicio was beyond hurt. "Why do people I love hit me like this! Why the fuck are so many games played with my mind?!"

"Felicio, I–."

"I was good without you, but you connected to me! Why ain't I worthy of love. Why are you abandon..." Felicio's words trailed off.

"I'm abandoning what?" Chanel said, tears rolling down her face.

"I'm not gonna let nobody do this to me again." She turned to walk away.

Chanel grabbed her hand. "What happened to you is not your fault."

"Fuck you talking about?" She snatched away.

"Your father left because he didn't deserve you. Not because you aren't worthy of love. And if I could be there for you right now I would."

"Fuck out my face."

"Please, don't leave like this," Chanel said.

Felicio looked down. "You know what...If this is what you want, so be it."

"It's not what I want. I just—."

"I got other shit on my mind, shawty."

"Chanel! Bring your ass back in here now!" Casey yelled out to her from the background.

Tears streamed down Chanel's face. She wiped them away harshly with the back of her hand.

"Go tend to your nigga." Felicio told her.

She walked away towards her truck. But as she got closer to the parking space, her heart sank when she realized her ride was no longer there.

"What the fuck? Where's my shit?" She muttered to herself, panic creeping into her voice.

She looked around, hoping to spot her beloved vehicle, but it was completely gone.

Vanished.

Felicio's mind raced with possibilities.

Had her truck been stolen?

It wasn't repossessed as her note had been paid up for a year.

When she looked above the space, the bitter reality hit her—she had parked in an area that she shouldn't have, and it must've been towed away.

The weight of her current situation settled heavily on her shoulders.

This was the absolute last thing she needed. She barely had money to survive on, she didn't have funds to be paying no fines.

Feeling defeated, Felicio took a deep breath, attempting to regain her composure. She knew she had to figure out a solution, but it felt like the world was closing in on her. She couldn't help but wonder if this was just another blow from a string of misfortunes.

With a heavy heart, no money, and no clue what to do, she turned back toward the house, ready to face the consequences of the argument and the harsh reality that her friendship with Chanel had ended abruptly.

As she approached the door, she steeled herself, prepared for whatever awaited her on the other side.

Knocking once, the door swung open, and she was faced to face with Casey. She said, "Look, man, I don't want no trouble, but my truck gone. I need a ride."

Casey looked at his girl then back at Felicio. He grabbed his keys and said, "I'll take you back to wherever the fuck you came from."

Felicio looked around him at Chanel who shook her head no before turning away and continuing to clean up the table.

Felicio weighed her options.

She didn't trust that this nigga wouldn't go crazy and try to do something to harm her.

"You know what, never mind. I'm good." She turned and walked away.

"Smart decision." Casey smirked before he slammed the door.

CHAPTER SEVENTEEN
HOBOSEXUAL SHIT

Felicio lay in bed, her body tense as she tried to find comfort in the unfamiliar embrace of the woman beside her.

A stranger.

Another broad she picked up, or who she allowed to pick her up just so she wouldn't have to sleep in the storage again.

Now this *was* some hobosexual shit.

The room was lit by candles and a small lamp, the smell of old fish drifted from the woman, intermingling with the stale odor of cigarettes.

Felicio was heated because like who still smoked cigarettes in 2023?

The woman, pretty and brown skinned with faux locs cascading down her back, exuded abrasiveness that Felicio found unsettling.

As the woman held a private conversation on her phone, her voice pierced through the silence of the room. It was loud and sharp, filled with a brazen disregard for anyone nearby.

Felicio winced, the yelling stinging her ears like shards of glass. "So, bitch I was like not uh, this is not enough money! My bundles cost way more than this. And she was giving broke, but she knew my prices before she even got there. Talking 'bout she wanted lemonade braids. I was like—"

Felicio bit the inside of her jaw.

She couldn't help but wrinkle her nose, trying to ignore the unpleasant combination assaulting her senses.

It was a contrast to the inviting aroma she had hoped for when she first met the woman at the lesbian lounge earlier that evening.

As the conversation on the phone continued, Felicio felt a growing sense of unease. This woman, with her attractive features and captivating presence, was simply not the right match for her.

The harshness of her words and the disdain in her tone revealed a side of her personality that clashed with Felicio's own desires for a place to lay her head.

Fuck this shit.

She quietly gathered her belongings, slipping into her clothes and tiptoeing towards the door.

"Hold on, Boobie! Tall M.A., I know you not about to slide out on me like that? Thought you was pulling up for the night." Stale Cig asked.

"Oh, yeah, naw, I gotta get up in a few hours so I should prolly hit it now." Felicio lied.

She didn't have anywhere to go and on top of that, she had no truck to get anywhere in, but she would rather sleep on the streets than to be in shawty's trap.

"But we ain't even get to have no fun yet." She said seductively.

Felicio wasn't wit' it, not even for a warm bed to lay in for the night. Especially if that bed had bally sheets that felt like crumbs with stains on them.

"Yeah, look ma, I got ya number and I know where you at. I'll pull up another night when I have more time to really enjoy you. How that sound?" Felicio was laying it on thick-thick, but she just really wanted to get out of there without drama.

"Mmm, I'm tight I ain't get to taste you, but definitely hit me when you free. Remember every Dom boy needs a little love. If you put it down I'ma pick it up up up!" She said raising her hand in the air and rocking her hips as if she were in the club and Doechii was on the stage.

Felicio blinked rapidly and smiled awkwardly before backing out the door.

As she stepped out into the cool night air, she took a deep breath, grateful to be free from the suffocating atmosphere of the room.

The sounds of the city enveloped her, drowning out the echoes of the woman's voice that played over in her mind.

She walked away, determined to sleep with rats in the storage before she spent another minute with a bird. She had run away from them before. This time they had better get out of her way.

Felicio stood outside her storage unit, the cool night air brushing against her skin.

The moon shone brightly overhead, casting a soft glow on the surroundings. The stars dotted the sky like shimmering diamonds, their radiance adding a touch of magic to the moment.

She gazed up at the celestial display when her phone buzzed in her hand.

It was Chanel.

With hesitation, Felicio answered the call. "What?"

"Hey," Chanel's voice greeted her on the other end.

"What's up, what you want?"

"I wanted to say sorry again about what happened with Casey. I know things got heated, and I didn't mean for it to go that far. Maybe we can still talk, you know over the phone or whatever?"

Felicio listened to Chanel's words, the sincerity in her voice seeping through. She glanced back at the storage unit, contemplating her response.

"Chanel," she began, her voice steady. "I appreciate the apology, I really do. But right now, I need some space. It's been a lot, and I need to figure things out on my own."

Chanel sighed on the other end of the line. "Aight, Felicio, I get it. Just know that I'm here for you, whenever you're ready to talk."

"But you not though, are you?"

"So you really gonna hold this against me? After everything?"

"Fuck you talking about?" Felicio scrunched her face up.

"What I'm talking about? Really?? I've been by your side since all this shit went down. Hell, even before that!"

"So now you throw it up in my face?"

"No...I just...I mean..."

"What do you want from me, shawty?" Felicio yelled. "Your nigga said stay away. So I'm staying the fuck away."

"You right."

"So what's up?"

"I called with that info."

"What info?"

"Zora's number."

"So you got it that quickly?"

"I been had it." Chanel's voice trailed off.

Felicio frowned. "Then why not give it to me before now?"

Chanel took her time to answer. "I needed an excuse to keep you around."

"So you did have your reasons? But since when do you need an excuse for me to be around you?"

Chanel realized how dumb it sounded. "I'm sorry."

"Man, that's the shit Casey prolly picked up on too." Felicio shook her head not sure what else to say about what she just found out.

"You got a pen?"

After recording the number Felicio said, "Thanks, man."

"Felicio, since we about to be on mute, I gotta tell you about April so you can be aware."

Silence.

"Felicio."

"What is it?"

"Like I told you, her father is Amish, and her mother was black. When she was little, he was shunned, and they lived together and raised her in an apartment in the projects in Baltimore." She sighed. "But he couldn't take what it was like living in a black community and being away from the place he called home all his life."

"How you know all this shit?"

"Oh, you know I'ma research queen. Part of her father's story was used in this white boy's college thesis on excommunicated Amish. The rest was public knowledge."

Felicio let out a deep breath, already over it. "Get to the point."

"Ok, please just hear me out."

She dragged a hand down her face. "Go 'head."

"So he was able to convince his family to let him back in and her mother raised her alone. The thing was she had sickle cell and when he left, it hit her hard. She had something called a pain crisis which led to a stroke and died."

Felicio stood up.

"When April moved to her new foster home she was just as confused. Number one, although she was black, they raised her wearing the traditional Amish clothing. Dresses to the ankles, things covering her hair and things of that nature. So now she's in a public school and not being homeschooled anymore and she's having all these weird feelings. She didn't really identify with the girls because she didn't feel girly. She didn't identify with the boys because she didn't feel like a boy. She was just confused. And violent."

"What you saying?"

"She had an obsession with a teacher. A woman who took her under her wing and let her stay in her home when she said they were mistreating her at her foster home. The woman tried to help her find out who she was inside, but all April wanted to do was lay up under her. So the woman let her until she fell in love."

Felicio walked outside and leaned against the wall by her storage.

"When the teacher met a mechanic, she told April she couldn't live there anymore. April was devastated, and a few days later when her new boyfriend was under a car in her teacher's yard, it came down on him and crushed his skull."

"Accidents happen."

"The teacher saw her do it and it threw her into depression. Missing her love and too afraid to tell the police, she walked out into traffic and died. Many years later, she met you."

Felicio was stunned. "I'm supposed to be scared?"

"You should be." Chanel sighed. "Some people can't handle having things taken away from them. She's one of them."

Felicio ended the call. "Fuck April and her story."

She pocketed her phone and turned her attention back to the night sky. The stars seemed to twinkle with a renewed brilliance.

And then she remembered...she finally had Zora's number.

So she made the call.

"Z..."

"New number, who this?"

Felicio chuckled, "You know who it is."

"How did you get my number?"

"Why? Do it matter?"

The phone went blank.

Felicio yelled, "Fuck!"

But it rang again, and she answered quickly.

"What do you want, Felicio?"

"Can I see you?"

"You been out for a minute. Why all of a sudden you wanna see me?"

Felicio didn't understand why she was mad when she was the one who abandoned her while in jail, but she let her go off.

"It took me a while to get your new number, man. Can we talk?"

Silence.

"Please."

"Yeah...whatever."

With an answer in tow, she took a final gaze up at the shimmering stars.

"Now it's time to destroy your ass, bitch." Felicio smirked, feeling vindictive.

CHAPTER EIGHTEEN
STALKER

Felicio walked into the lively bar as rap music thumped throughout. The dark space was filled with laughter, chatter, and the clinking of glasses.

She scanned the room, her eyes landing on a familiar face at a corner booth—Zora, her friend whom she intended to rescue from April's clutches.

Making her way through the crowd, Felicio was approaching the booth where Zora sat, engrossed in conversation on the phone. As she neared, she noticed the aroma of freshly baked pizza wafting through the air, making her stomach growl in anticipation.

"What up, Z," Felicio called out, sliding into the booth beside her.

The sound of Latto's, *'Put It On Da Floor'* blared in the background, adding a vibrant energy to the atmosphere.

Zora's eyes lit up as she ended her call and turned to face Felicio. "Hey…you look good. Like you been holding up."

Felicio nodded; her attention momentarily drawn to the mouthwatering pizza laid out before them. The slices were generously topped with an assortment of colorful ingredients, from savory meats to vibrant vegetables.

She couldn't resist grabbing a slice and taking a bite.

"Help yourself!" Zora joked.

Felicio laughed.

Between bites, Felicio broached the topic that had brought her there. "So, Z, I heard you the real mastermind behind April's new online business. How's it going?"

Zora frowned. "That's what you wanna talk about first?"

"What? I'm just asking." Felicio said chewing.

Zora took a sip of her martini.

"Well, it's growing. I set the website up and got everything running smoothly. I never thought I'd find success in the foot fetish market, but here we are. April was right."

Felicio angry chewed. "Now let's talk about how you let April come in between us."

"Wait...what?"

"You abandoned me in jail." Felicio said, displaying how her feelings were hurt.

"You really are serious."

"Yeah. I ain't expect that shit from none of y'all for real for real, but definitely not you." She swallowed.

"You were the one who told us not to come up there. You were the one who tried to get us hemmed up." Zora spat.

"Wait...that's Cap! Who told you that shit?"

Silence.

"Z, who the fuck told—?" Felicio stopped mid question realizing she already knew the answer. "It was April's psychotic ass. Wasn't it?"

Since shit was getting serious in the booth, Felicio couldn't help but wish they turned the trap music down in the bar.

"Yeah, it was her." Zora admitted.

Her temples flared. "You think I would ever do that to you? To any of y'all? We may have a weird family situation, but I loved y'all. Seeing you would've been exactly what I needed."

Zora realized how dumb it sounded and felt bad immediately. "Wow."

"And you let her do that shit by throwing space between us when I been knowing you longer?"

Zora felt guilty but had to defend herself. "Yes, I admit I did but I was also the one who paid up your storage for a year. I was the one who made sure your truck note was paid up for a year too and your cell phone, and insurance, since we making a list. So despite what I thought you did, I still looked out." She looked down. "Pulled out all my money and it's the reason I need April's business now."

Felicio was shocked.

She closed her eyes and took a deep breath. She was relieved that at least she was a good judge of character where Zora was concerned.

She had always been solid.

Of course she paid her shit off. Who else would it have been? Chanel was in jail too plus she would have told her had she been responsible.

"I'm sorry, I appreciate that you looked out too."

Zora gave her a half smile accepting her apology.

"How's Khari?"

"She's gotten sicker. The business is helping me pay her bills 'cause she's not really been able to work much. And it's helping me get my bag back up."

Felicio sat back.

This may put a hitch in the revenge plan to snatch Zora. She didn't want to do anything that would jeopardize Khari getting the medical help that she needed. And she didn't want Zora in any more binds.

So she decided right then to back away from that angle and come up with another plan.

Outside the crowded bar in the Adams Morgan area of DC, the night air enveloped Felicio and Zora as they stepped onto the sidewalk to have a few more words.

The streetlights cast a warm glow, illuminating the path before them. The sounds of distant traffic and muffled conversations from nearby establishments filled the air.

Felicio turned to Zora, her eyes filled with concern. "Zora, I really want you to be careful with April. She's not to be trusted. I've seen her true colors, and I don't want her dragging you down."

Zora nodded, her brow furrowing with apprehension. "I hear you, Felicio. I know things have gotten messy, and it's hard to trust anyone right now. But I'ma ask her about all this shit. Believe that!"

"It's deeper than that...I learned some more stuff and I want you to look out for yourself. And Khari too."

As Felicio walked Zora to her car, unbeknownst to them, April, with her piercing gaze and simmering jealousy, sat across the street, silently seething with anger watching them. Her eyes burned with envy, and a growing desire for vengeance.

The night wrapped around Felicio and Zora as they said their goodbyes, unaware of the storm brewing just beyond their line of sight.

CHAPTER NINETEEN
TRUE COLORS

In the small confines of their shared living room, April and Zora sat on opposite ends of the tattered couch.

The flickering glow of a muted TV cast long shadows across the room, adding an air of tension to their conversation.

April fidgeted with the frayed edge of her hoodie, her eyes darting nervously towards Zora. She could sense the weight of suspicion hanging heavy in the air, threatening to shatter the bond they had built over time.

Zora's voice broke the uneasy silence.

"April, we need to talk. I can't ignore the rumors anymore."

April was livid but she tried to maintain calm. "What is it? Because it looks like you already got your mind made up."

"Why did you lie about Felicio not wanting to see us when she got locked up?"

April shifted a little. "I mean...I..."

"Did you set Felicio up? Did you betray her?" Zora's voice was steady, but her eyes held a hint of disappointment.

"I don't get it."

"A simple question?"

April's heart skipped a beat, her mind racing for the right words.

She shifted uneasily in her seat, desperately trying to find a way to salvage their friendship. "Zora, you know I would never do something like that."

"Do I know?"

"Wow."

"Did you betray her?"

"You know how much Felicio meant to me. She was my friend too, and I would never betray her trust."

Zora's gaze hardened. Suspicion etched on her face. "But people saying that you had a hand in her getting locked up."

"People?"

"Yeah."

"People like Felicio?"

She ignored her inquiry. "They say you set her up and turned your back on her. Is any of that true? No more games!"

April's voice trembled slightly as she vehemently denied the accusations. "No, Zora, it's not true. I would never do something so low."

"But you hate her."

"I hate her now."

"What happened that night you walked in after getting a call while we were all on the bed?"

"What you talking about?"

"Did you see her that night? Because things changed when you came back."

"What...no!"

"You were upset about something."

"Listen, Felicio was important to me, and I've always had her back. I don't know where these 'so called' rumors are coming from, but I swear they fake."

Zora leaned back, her brows furrowed in contemplation. She couldn't shake off the nagging doubts that had crept into her mind. The weight of uncertainty hung in the room.

Zora's voice wavered as she spoke about her concerns.

"I want to say something to you, and I don't want you to take it wrong. You don't have to respond, I'm just going to get it out. I see you around people. I see you around and it's like you're fighting to fit into one category or another. You don't feel straight. You don't feel gay. You don't like to wear only girl clothes. You don't like to wear only boy clothing. And I think I know what's going on."

"Nothing's wrong with me." Her eyes were large and scary.

"I don't like labels. But I saw you watching the show the other day. When they were interviewing that girl who identified as THEY. All I want to say is if something is on your heart and you need to talk, I'll understand. This is the moment to be who you really are. And I won't have any judgment on you. don't let this moment go by."

"There's nothing wrong with me! just because I am not the kind of lesbian that you–"

"I don't even think you are lesbian! You said it yourself you hate when people just think girls are supposed to dress one way and boys are supposed to dress another. Maybe you should–"

"Even if there was something wrong why would I come to you? You make fun of me. Don't drop shit when I ask for it to be dropped, all for fun?"

"What you talking about?"

"The man in the club."

"I—"

"Don't fuck with me! I'm warning you!" She paused. "Like I said I'll be okay."

"April, I want to believe you. I really do."

"Then believe me."

"But there are too many doubts. Something doesn't add up, and I can't ignore it anymore. I need to know the truth right here and right now."

April's eyes glistened with frustration and hurt. She reached out to touch Zora's arm, her voice pleading. "I'm being straight up, Zora, please just trust me."

She took a minute before she answered. "I need time."

"But I've been honest with you from the beginning. Felicio was my friend, and I would never do anything to hurt her. And me, you and Khari been through so much together. Don't let these rumors tear us apart."

Zora pulled away, conflicted.

"Zora, say something."

"I said I need time, April. Time to process all of this. Our friendship...it's hanging by a thread right now."

Her heart sank as she watched Zora rise from the couch, the room would surely grow cold in her absence.

She reached out to grab Zora's hand, her voice filled with desperation.

"Zora, please don't go. Don't leave me! I'm begging you."

Zora pulled her hand back and walked down the hall.

"We can work this out together! I need you by my side, now more than ever!"

Zora stopped and turned around. Her eyes met April's, the bond of their friendship momentarily flickering before dimming once again.

"You gotta make shit right."

"What's that mean?"

"With all of us."

April stared at her intensely.

"Where were you tonight?" She asked, ignoring her declaration.

Silence.

April stood up. "Bitch, I asked you a question. I'm tired of faking nice with you."

Zora shook her head. "Faking nice?" She chuckled. "I knew it. You changed, or maybe I'm just now seeing the real you." She walked back toward her. "Check this out, I'm not your girlfriend and don't have to answer any of your questions about my whereabouts. Fuck off!" She turned around and walked out the living room again.

Silence hung heavy in the room as Zora's footsteps faded into the darkness.

April was left alone, grappling with the shattered fragments of trust that lay scattered all around her.

She rubbed her hand down her face harshly and blew breath out of her mouth angrily.

"That fucking Felicio! I can't wait to bury her once and for all." She said to herself before she flopped back on the couch.

CHAPTER TWENTY
GETBACK

The setting sun bathed the city in a warm, golden hue, casting long shadows that stretched across the pavement.

April's knuckles turned white as she gripped the steering wheel of the rented U-Haul, her eyes fixed on the road ahead. The wet streets amplified the intensity of her emotions, as if the scene mirrored the anger simmering within her.

She drove intensely with pure hate in her heart.

Her mind buzzed with a flurry of thoughts, each one a calculated piece of her plan falling into place.

She knew that revenge required careful plotting, and she was determined to execute her scheme flawlessly.

Earlier, in the mall, April had entered a store, the smell of new merchandise filling her senses.

She walked in, duffel bags in hand, their sturdy fabric promising secrecy and concealment. As she clutched the bags tightly, a shiver of anticipation ran down her spine, knowing they held what she needed to exact her revenge.

She left out lighter and satisfied.

Now, back in the driver's seat of the U-Haul, April's eyes flickered with defiance and determination.

Suddenly her phone buzzed, the screen lighting up with Khari's name.

KHARI:
Can you stop past the Rite Aid on your way back and pick up my prescription please?

But in that moment, her anger prevailed.

"Fuck no! Get it yourself." She said out loud before deleting the message.

Her illness reminded her of weakness. Of a mother too weak to take care of her, leaving her alone. The type of pain she felt was too heavy to acknowledge and so she didn't.

With a turn of the key, the engine roared to life, the sound resonating through the empty streets.

April's foot pressed firmly on the pedal as the U-Haul accelerated, its tires gripping the asphalt with a sense of purpose.

After leaving the post office, the place where April had all their mail forwarded from the old apartment, she sat alone in the truck.

She held the suspicious letter in her trembling hands, her eyes scanning the words written on the wrinkled paper. The envelope bore no return address, leaving her with a chilling sense of unease.

As she unfolded the letter, her heart quickened its pace, as if anticipating the weight of the message it contained.

The inked words sprawled across the page, their jagged edges and uneven spacing adding to the ominous atmosphere that engulfed her.

'What you did was wrong, April,' the letter began, each word etched with an unsettling intensity. *'You thought you could escape the consequences, but remember, karma always finds its way back to those who seek to manipulate and deceive.'*

A chill ran down April's spine as she read those words, the gravity of their meaning sinking deep into her consciousness.

As April reached the final lines of the letter, her breath caught in her throat. *'Be prepared, for what you sow shall be your harvest. The seeds of your actions have been planted, and soon they will sprout, bringing forth a bounty of consequences you can't escape.'*

Fear tightened its grip around April's heart.

This letter fucked her all the way up.

The realization that her past misdeeds were catching up to her filled her with a sense of impending doom.

It brought her face-to-face with the consequences she had so willingly ignored, leaving her trembling with apprehension.

The once-clear path ahead now seemed clouded and treacherous, with no certainty of what lay in wait.

"Fuck!" She yelled and hit the steering wheel.

CHAPTER TWENTY-ONE
FUEGO

Felicio stood in the middle of her storage unit, her eyes wide with shock and disbelief.

ALL HER SHIT WAS GONE!

The once familiar space that had housed her belongings, her memories, and her temporary refuge was now an empty shell, stripped bare by the cruel hands of a thief.

The realization hit her like a punch to the gut, leaving her breathless and overwhelmed.

Every trace of her existence was gone, taken away without mercy.

The tennis shoes she had painstakingly collected, the few remnants of comfort and familiarity in her tumultuous life, were now in the hands of an unknown culprit. Anger and despair welled up within her, threatening to consume her fragile state of mind.

Her shoes had been her constant companions, providing a sense of comfort and familiarity.

As she gazed upon the vacant space where her cherished sneaks had once resided, her heart sank to her feet.

But it wasn't just her precious shoes and clothes that were taken, this thief snatched everything!

Even her makeshift bed.

Like what the fuck they want with that?

Amidst the emptiness, a solitary note lay on the floor, as if it mocked her.

Felicio's trembling hands reached down to pick it up, her eyes scanning the message scrawled upon it.

The words etched in April's handwriting pierced through her soul, a venomous reminder of the consequences of their tangled web of revenge.

You never should have fucked with me.

Those words stayed on repeat in Felicio's mind, as if they were haunting her.

The weight of her actions hit her like a smack in the face.

In her quest for vengeance, she had not only lost her material possessions but also compromised her own well-being.

Chanel warned her and she didn't heed.

With a heavy heart, Felicio stepped out of the vacant storage unit, into the scarcely lit street.

The world around her seemed to match the darkness that now took over her spirit.

On top of that, the sky opened up, releasing a torrent of rain that soaked her army green raincoat, the droplets mingling with the tears that streamed down her tattooed face.

Under the flickering streetlight, Felicio stood, her body trembling with exhaustion and despair.

Her once resilient spirit wavered, teetering on the edge of hopelessness and the verge of giving the fuck up.

She questioned the choices she had made, the paths she had chosen, and the consequences they had brought upon her.

She realized she may have gone too far left.

Suddenly the rain that drenched her served as a baptism, washing away the remnants of her past and felt like it could've been cleansing her spirit.

She sat in the uncomfortableness and really debated walking away from it all.

But in the battle of good versus evil that was happening in her mind in that moment, evil's ass won.

Felicio took a step forward and it was settled. She would rise from the ashes and rebuild her life by drinking on April's blood.

By C. WASH

As she walked into the unknown, another idea struck her.

If she carried this out, it would change everything.

But she didn't give a fuck anymore.

Why should she?

The rain poured down harder, its rhythm echoing throughout her heart.

The gloves were off, it was time to fight dirty.

Chanel's car pulled up to the curb as she searched for her friend.

She stepped out of the vehicle and noticed Felicio standing near the entrance of the building, weariness all over her face.

Their eyes met, and a surge of emotions washed over Chanel—relief, concern, and a lingering sense of guilt.

Without hesitation, Felicio approached her, the weight of her circumstances evident in her every step. She mustered a small smile, though her eyes displayed the fatigue she carried.

"Hey, Chanel," she greeted, her voice tinged with vulnerability and gratitude.

Chanel opened her arms wide, embracing Felicio in a heartfelt hug. It was a moment of reconciliation, a silent acknowledgment that their bond transcended any conflicts or misunderstandings that had come between them.

"I'm so sorry, Felicio," Chanel whispered. "I'm sorry for letting anyone come between us. I missed you so much."

Felicio's grip tightened momentarily, the closeness offering a sense of comfort in the midst of her hardships.

"I'm glad you answered my call, shawty. I didn't know what else to do or where to turn." She said into her ear while still locked in an embrace.

Chanel held onto her for dear life and let her get everything off her chest.

"She took everything, everything from me. I got nothing left, nothing." Felicio confessed on the verge of a breakdown.

Chanel hated to hear the despair and agony in her voice. She wanted to do anything that she could to make her feel better.

She pulled away slightly, her gaze entangled with Felicio's. Then suddenly she stood up on her tip toes and kissed her.

The kiss was passionate yet gentle and felt like a long time coming.

Felicio was so distraught she seemed to melt into the affection. Her body yearned for the connection.

The heat got turned up while they continued to kiss as their tongues found their way into each other's mouths.

Although Chanel started this encounter off to make her feel better, Felicio began to rejuvenate and take charge.

She used her body to back Chanel over to her car and pinned her against the back door with their lips still intertwined and began to move her hands all over the soft curves of her body.

As she explored her breasts and hips and around her ass, she found a home under her body con dress on the hunt for her waiting pussy.

She reached what she searched for and the only thing standing in the way of sliding up into her opening were a pair of lace thongs.

She moved them to the side and continued her exploration.

Her knees almost buckled when she felt how wet Chanel's pussy was. Her juices saturated her fingers like expensive oil.

She let out a soft moan informing Felicio that she was enjoying her touch as Felicio began to finger fuck her with precision.

In this moment, they didn't think about April, or Casey or even whoever could see their PDA on the street. This moment was about them and them only.

But just as Felicio was about to kick this scene up a notch, Chanel pulled her head back from the kiss harshly. A look of pain etched throughout her face.

"OOoooooouuuccchhhhh!! What the fuck?" She screamed shaking her legs back and forth and stomping her feet.

"What's wrong, girl?" Felicio stood up straight and asked as she watched her wriggle around in front of her.

"My pussy is on fire! What the fuck? Why is my pussy burning like that?"

"What you mean it's burning?" Felicio asked in disbelief.

"I mean it's burning like somebody poured hot sauce into me, ugggghhhhh." She yelled and continued to dance around the sidewalk.

Felicio's face was contorted into a scowl and then instantaneously, she knew what happened.

On her way back to the storage unit she was hungry but only had a few dollars to eat. So she stopped and grabbed a bag of red Taki's and a Gatorade for the long walk.

She crushed the bag right before she arrived at her unit without having a chance to clean her hands.

She entered Chanel's pussy with *Fuego Taki* dusted fingertips.

"Oh my God, Chanel I'm so sorry!" She blurted out feeling guilty. "I was eating Taki's earlier and hadn't washed my hands yet."

"Taki's...Taki's!!" Chanel yelled sounding like Soldier Boy on the Breakfast Club when he kept repeating the name Drake.

"My bad, boo." Felicio covered her mouth in an attempt to hold back the laughter she tried to control.

Chanel, who was still visibly in pain began to laugh too.

"I gotta get some water on this before I pass out. Let's go someplace else."

THIRTY MINUTES LATER

After coming out of the shower in a towel, Chanel joined Felicio on the couch in the living room.

She was at her sister's apartment who lived not too far from the storage facility. She was happy her sister, who was normally at work, was home to let her in.

Felicio waited for Chanel to speak before she said anything.

"Nigga, that shit almost took me out!" She stated. "I thought I would have to go to the hospital!"

"And what the fuck was you gonna say when you got there?" Felicio asked, chuckling.

"Who knows! But I do know I would have been the laughingstock of that place." Chanel dropped her head.

"How you feeling now?"

"Better, kind of numb but not burning no more." Chanel shook her head.

"Man, that's probably a sign that we shouldn't have been doing that." Felicio admitted.

"Please, the only thing that was a sign of is wash your hands before you get to finger popping." Chanel laughed.

Felicio chuckled and then grew serious.

"I missed your crazy ass, shawty."

"I missed you too, boo." She smiled. "So, what can I do to help?"

"I need your car for a little while, and…a few bucks would help too," she admitted, her tone both vulnerable and determined.

Chanel nodded, her heart swelling with empathy. "You can have whatever you need." She handed over the key without hesitation and dug into her purse to retrieve a twenty-dollar bill.

"Thank you, I'll bring it back as soon as I can."

"Bring back yourself instead."

Felicio winked.

"Take care of whatever you need to, Felicio," Chanel said softly, her voice filled with genuine concern.

Felicio swallowed the lump in her throat.

"I'm here for you. Always." Chanel reassured her.

"Before I leave, can you get me April's new address?"

"Been had it. Stay right here." She returned a few moments later and handed it to her.

"You wild as shit."

"Anything for you."

A bittersweet smile graced Felicio's lips as she leaned in and kissed her softly. It was a kiss not laced with passion, but more like an understanding of possibilities to come.

CHAPTER TWENTY-TWO
CONFRONTATIONS

Felicio's grip tightened on the steering wheel as she pulled up to the address she had been given.

It was early in the morning and only the dew on the grass was out in the neighborhood.

She knew she may have to wait awhile before she could get what she came for and with nothing else to lose, she threw the car in park and did just that.

TWO HOURS LATER

When Felicio awoke from her unintended slumber, she recognized the man currently playing with his son in the sandbox from the club.

Over seven months ago, he was the guy who got into it with April on the dancefloor.

Sitting there parked in Chanel's Benz on the quiet street, she took a moment to collect herself. The weight of the past months pressed heavily on her shoulders, but she was determined to confront the truth, whatever it may be.

Taking a deep breath, she stepped out the car and made her way towards the gated entrance.

The man, his broad shoulders and strong presence commanding attention, noticed Felicio's arrival. He turned and a hint of recognition flickered in his eyes as he watched her approach.

The sounds of the child playing filled the air as if all hell wasn't possibly about to break loose.

Felicio reached the gate and locked eyes with him, her gaze unwavering.

"I'm not here for no drama." She started. "But we gotta talk," she said, her voice tinged with determination. The words hung in the air, carrying a sense of urgency and a yearning for answers.

A nod of acknowledgment passed between them, and the man motioned for Felicio to enter.

Inside, the atmosphere shifted. The sound of laughter faded, replaced by a tense silence that seemed to cover the space.

The walls whispered secrets, and Felicio could feel the weight of the untold story hovering over her like a cloud.

By C. WASH

Her eyes darted around the room, searching for clues, for any hint of the truth she so desperately sought.

The man turned to face her, "I'm not sure how much you know, but I have a feeling a lot of light is about to be shed onto both of us." He said, his voice laced with a hint of mystery that left Felicio yearning for more.

The room seemed to hold its breath as they stood there, on the precipice of a revelation.

But what secrets were about to be unraveled?

April was walking around plotting more revenge on Felicio when suddenly her front door came crashing open.

The atmosphere in the apartment shifted from calm to a charged intensity as the man from the club entered.

His eyes blazed with anger and betrayal, his presence filling the room with an unsettling energy. April and Khari, the only two currently in their apartment, exchanged glances between each other, their hearts racing with fear and confusion.

"What the fuck have you done to us?" The man growled, his voice heavy with anger.

April was stunned.

How did he know where she lived?

How did he find her?

"When I mailed you that letter and didn't hear anything, I just knew I wouldn't be able to find you." He glared harder. "Guess I was wrong."

"What you doing here!"

"I trusted you, April. I trusted you with our child's future."

Khari's mouth dropped open at the revelation.

April's mind raced, her thoughts colliding in a chaotic whirlwind. She had kept this relationship and her child hidden from her friends, never expecting that her secrets would come exploding upon her like this.

Until she remembered Felicio being with her one day at a restaurant. She had gone to the bathroom, and when she returned the man was going off on April. He left before Felicio could step to him.

But she heard everything.

"You got a kid?" Felicio asked.

April said yes but that it was complicated.

So Felicio left it alone.

Now he was in her home. Her personal space, with hate in his eyes. Panic gripped her as she struggled to find the right words, her voice trembling.

"I... I didn't mean for things to turn out this way," April stammered, her voice barely above a whisper. "I needed the money; I thought I could pay it back once my new business was up and running successfully, but it's taking longer to lift off like I hoped. I never meant to hurt our child."

The stranger's eyes narrowed; his fists clenched at his sides. "You stole fifty thousand dollars! Most of the money I put in!"

She had used it to fake rich for the apartment until the money ran out. And now she was caught.

"I'm so fucking sorry!"

"You think that apology is gonna make up for the damage you've done? For the trust you've shattered?" His words hung heavy in the air, each syllable dripping with pain.

Khari, usually the calm and collected one, stepped forward, her voice laced with a firm resolve. "Look, I don't know about any of this, but you can't be here."

"Stay out of it!" He roared at her.

"Listen, I can't let you hurt my friend." She continued.

"Birds of a fucking feather." He looked her up and down with haste.

As they continued to yell, April's eyes darted between the two, with guilt, fear, and regret all dancing across her face.

She had kept her secrets hidden, believing she could protect herself from everyone knowing. But now the consequences of her actions were unfolding in front of her, unraveling the carefully constructed facade she had built.

She wanted to run and leave Khari alone, but he was blocking the door.

"I'm sorry," April whispered, her voice choking with emotion. "I was desperate, and I made a terrible mistake."

The stranger's anger seemed to momentarily subside, replaced by a heavy weariness. He let out a sigh, the tension in the room easing slightly. "Our child, our son, deserves better, April. He deserves to have a stable future, to be cared for and protected."

April became consumed with anger when she thought back to how this all happened in the first place.

Growing up, April was a tall, lanky awkward teenage girl who wasn't sure of who she was when she started going to public school.

She wasn't into boys, and with her being the tallest person in her class, they weren't into her. On the flip side, at that time, she wasn't necessarily gay yet either, but she had a better shot at girls than she did with guys, so that's who she pursued.

However, it was always something.

She was either too soft for the Fem's who wanted Dom's and too Dom for the girls that wanted Fem's.

Once again, she was left wanting.

So she swore off women, and tried her long hand out on men, again. For the most part, she was still rejected. Until she met a man in the bar, and they began playing 20 questions for shots.

They got so drunk, they fucked, and she ended up pregnant.

But slim ain't want to be with her, in his mind she was a one nighter, and he definitely didn't want a baby.

Now, instead of having an abortion, she decided to keep the kid, thinking that a baby may be cool to have to love on. But when her son got here and she couldn't take single parenthood, she threatened her baby daddy with either taking the kid himself or she would put him on child support.

He reluctantly decided to raise their son himself under one stipulation, that she would come see him every now and again and that they open an account that they both put money into for his future.

That was the plan.

But, once April found the website, *LOP* and realized she could be anybody she wanted there, she no longer wanted to play mommy.

Not even part time.

Tiring of his ranting, and in the true to form of her bipolarness she said, "You know what, fuck you and that kid!"

"What did you just say?"

"Nigga, you heard me! Coming over here busting up in my shit like you God.

You ain't God! You just mad cause I didn't wanna be with y'all. You thought me having that kid was gonna trap me, but no!" She continued to go off. "I was entitled to that money! I put half of it in myself."

She was delusional.

In that moment, he realized how narcissistic she was and without warning, he charged her and beat her repeatedly about the face.

Khari's eyes widened in fear.

The room erupted with a chorus of raised voices, anger and frustration swirling in the air as the dude continued to lose his mind all over April's ass.

But in the midst of their tumultuous fight, a sudden, agonizing cry pierced through the chaos.

Khari's face contorted in pain as she clutched her chest, her eyes bulging in sheer panic. The color drained from her cheeks, as beads of sweat formed on her brow. It was as if time froze, the room hushed, and everyone's attention shifted to the distress unfolding before them.

He pulled himself off of April's bloody body.

Khari struggled to speak, gasping for breath as the pain tightened its grip on her chest. Her body trembled, and she collapsed onto the floor, unable to withstand the intensity of the heart attack that had suddenly seized her.

The man's eyes widened as he ran for the door. "You're gonna pay me my money, bitch! Believe that!"

Suddenly a neighbor entered.

"I heard the screams! The ambulance is on the way."

Khari continued to grip her chest and April passed out.

Minutes felt like an eternity as they waited for the paramedics to arrive. The room was consumed by a thick silence, punctuated only by the sound of Khari's labored breathing and the distant wailing of sirens growing steadily louder.

This looked like the end.

CHAPTER TWENTY-THREE
GUILT GUT PUNCH

Felicio hastily parked Chanel's Benz, not bothering with precision, as her mind was consumed with worry and urgency.

She dashed out of the car and hurried into the hospital, her heart pounding in her chest.

The scent of disinfectant permeated the air, mingling with the sounds of hurried footsteps and distant medical chatter.

Without taking a moment to compose herself, Felicio approached the reception desk, her voice trembling with anxiety.

"Khari Williams?" She stood stuck waiting for the nurse to provide the information she sought after.

"Uh yes, she's in room 211, right down there." The hospital personnel stated, and she took off through the maze-like corridors, determined to reach her friend's side.

Her desperation grew with each passing second, and she couldn't help but feel a pang of guilt for not being there when Khari needed her the most.

Finally, Felicio arrived at Khari's room, breathless and filled with apprehension.

Upon entering, relief washed over her when she saw Zora by Khari's bedside. Zora's eyes widened in surprise as she noticed Felicio's disheveled appearance.

"Felicio, you made it," Zora said, with concern in her voice. She hugged her tightly. "What took you so long?"

"I got here as fast as I could." She paused. "Is everything alright? I mean what happened?" Felicio's chest heaved as she tried to catch her breath, her eyes darting between Zora and Khari.

"She had a flare up that they think caused a heart attack. They said it's not common, but it can happen." She paused and looked at her intensely. "Were you responsible? For any of this?"

Felicio looked down, guilt gut punching her. "I'll explain later, Zora," she managed to say between gasps for air. "Right now, we need to be here for Khari."

Zora nodded, sensing the urgency in Felicio's voice. They set aside their questions for the time being their focus shifting entirely to their ailing friend lying in the hospital bed.

Pulling up chairs beside Khari, Felicio and Zora settled in, their presence offering a small measure of comfort amidst the sterile hospital environment.

As they sat there, a heaviness filled the room, the unspoken questions lingering between them.

Felicio leaned in closer, her voice barely above a whisper. "How long have things gotten worse for her health?"

"Honestly?"

"Yeah."

"It started getting bad right around when you left."

"But I thought the business was making things easier for her." Felicio asked. "Due to meds."

"She's stressed the fuck out. I mean why wouldn't she be?" Zora said honestly.

"We gonna get her through this." Felicio reassured. "I'ma be real, I can't fuck with April no more. But I hope after you hear everything, we can still get back to us."

"I don't know. For real I don't." Zora said. "Because too much has happened too fast, and I don't know who or what to believe anymore."

Felicio nodded, understanding the need to prioritize their friend's well-being over seeking immediate answers.

Together, they sat vigil by Khari's side, minutes turning into hours as they waited for any signs of improvement.

Thirty minutes later she said, "Now we have to talk."

Felicio told her about what April had done in more detail to get her arrested. She told her about her mother and her past and the mechanic under the car. She even told her that she thought her life was in danger.

In the end Zora said, "That explains so much."

"Like what?"

"Because she doesn't know who she is, she has a strong obsession to connect herself with people who know who they are."

"The fucked up part is I'm still figuring my shit out," Felicio admitted.

"Me too. All of us are. But she's too fucked up to get that."

"But listen…while we going through this, and you still living in that apartment with her, don't eat or drink anything you haven't opened yourself."

"You think she'll go that far?" She asked slightly trembling.

"Actually…I do."

CHAPTER TWENTY-FOUR
REVELATION

Chanel pulled up to the hotel, the engine of her Benz humming softly as she waited for Felicio to walk out.

Felicio emerged, feeling a bit of exhaustion and relief after a fitful night's sleep.

As she approached the car, Chanel handed her a steaming cup of coffee and a warm Egg McMuffin.

"Breakfast of champions," Chanel said with a playful smile, gesturing to the food in Felicio's hands. "I figured we could use some fuel for the day ahead."

Felicio gratefully accepted the offerings, the aroma of the coffee mingling with the scent of freshly baked bread.

She took a sip, feeling the warmth spread through her body, rejuvenating her senses. "Thanks, Shawty. You always know how to take care of me."

As they settled into the car, Chanel started the engine and turned to Felicio. "So, here's the plan for today," she began, her voice laced with excitement. "First, we grab lunch at that new soul food joint across town. And later, I thought we could catch a movie or something. I just want to try and get your mind off things for a while. What do you say?"

Felicio nodded, grateful for Chanel's thoughtfulness and the distraction from the heaviness that weighed on her heart. "That sounds perfect. Spending time with you always lifts my spirits. But I have something else to do first."

Chanel's eyes softened, and she glanced at Felicio, her voice becoming more vulnerable. "I have something I wanna confess."

"Shoot."

Chanel looked between her and the road. "After what happened between us the other night and everything we've been through, I've come to realize that my feelings for you run deeper than just friendship. I care about you more than I can put into words."

Felicio's heart skipped a beat, her mind racing with many emotions.

She had always valued Chanel's presence in her life, but the thought of romantic entanglements seemed both thrilling and overwhelming. She reached out and placed a reassuring hand on Chanel's leg.

"I appreciate your honesty," Felicio replied, her voice filled with sincerity. "You mean a lot to me too, more than you know and I value our friendship above anything." She took a deep breath. "But I realize I ain't work on my own shit. I rely on you so much that I forgot you can't rely on me. And I wanna change that I just gotta get unstuck."

"What you mean?"

"When my father left me, it fucked me up...it still fucks me up. And I don't like how I am with that kind of mindset. I gotta...I gotta be clear about how I'm moving in life before we see what this could be. I wouldn't want to jump in face first and it don't work out then I lose my homie. Feel me?"

Chanel nodded, "I completely understand. Take all the time you need. I'm here for you, no matter what."

"That don't mean I want you getting no new nigga." She chuckled once. "I just want you to give me some time."

"I hear you. And I feel you."

"Cool...take me to the hospital. I gotta see about my friend."

"No problem."

Twenty minutes later the car pulled into the hospital parking lot.

As they made their way inside, their conversation shifted to concern for Khari's well-being, their own emotions momentarily put on pause.

Together, they strolled down the sterile corridors, their footsteps echoing in the quiet hallways. The weight of the situation hung in the air, but with Chanel by her side, she found strength and solace.

"I'll wait out here." Chanel said before kissing her on the cheek.

Felicio nodded.

As she entered Khari's room, once again she hoped she was awake but resigned to her still being in a coma.

She sat next to her bed and grabbed her hand.

"Khari, I'm so sorry I haven't been there for you. I need you to know that you mean the world to me, and I promise to help you get back on your feet. No matter how long it takes, I got you. Just shake back, friend, please."

Felicio didn't care how long it took.

When Khari woke up, she would be there.

Never abandoning her.

She said a silent prayer over her and stood up.

She knew then that it was time to go to her next destination.

Alone.

Felicio stood at the doorway of April and Zora's apartment, her expression a blend of determination and weariness.

She took a deep breath, readying herself for what lay ahead. With a resolve to end the ongoing feud and forge a new path, she stepped inside, her eyes scanning the space for her former friend.

April, seething with anger, stood in the center of the room, her face beaten and bludgeoned to the gods. And her eyes ablaze with fury.

Zora, after letting Felicio in, walked over to the couch and sat down.

"Well, well, well...what do you wanna talk about?" April asked.

Felicio locked eyes with Zora, silently acknowledging the weight of their shared experiences and the bond that had grown between them.

She threw her hands in the air. "I'm done fighting, April," Felicio declared, her voice firm yet tinged with a touch of sadness.

"So you done huh? Just like that...All of a sudden?"

"We've hurt each other enough, and someone we both care about got injured in the process too. It's time to put an end to this shit."

April scoffed, her voice dripping with disdain. "I don't give a fuck about Khari or anybody else," she retorted, her anger radiating through every word. "And that nigga beating me up? That's your fault for meddling in my business."

"You mean your baby father?"

"I didn't have to tell you or anybody everything about my past."

"But you claimed you were a lesbian." Zora added. "And you right, you didn't have to tell us but why lie about having a son?"

"Fuck you and you!" April continued pointing a chipped nail their way.

Zora, her patience worn thin, interjected, her voice filled with disappointment. "April, this is exactly what I'm talking about. You so focused on yourself that you fail to see the consequences of your own shit. You took advantage of your own child, and now you don't even care about Khari's well-being? I can't be friends with someone so selfish anymore. I won't!"

April's rage intensified, her voice raising in volume as she unleashed her fury upon her former friends.

"You know what...I don't give a fuck! Y'all are a gaggle of ungrateful bitches and I'm sick of you anyway! When this nigga got locked up, I held us down." She pointed at Felicio. "Did you forget that?" April spat.

"First of all, had your bitch ass never called the PoPo I wouldn't have gotten locked up! We was doing good with the business I implemented. Niggas was eating and had good money in they pockets, but all you saw was trying to take over the operation and run it yourself. I'm mad I didn't see that shit until it was too late." Felicio shouted.

"That's right, everybody ain't built to sell drugs. Shit, part of the reason I started taking the kid's money was because I had to pay you for my portion of the pills that I took myself because y'all were stressing me the fuck out."

"Took yourself?" Zora said. "Are you crazy?"

"No...I'm not!"

Felicio and Zora's eyes widened after her declaration.

"Wowwwww...." Felicio was blown away.

"And I called the police on you because you never respected me, you were threatened by me. All you cared about was them Fem bitches, you never really saw me!" April shouted.

Zora couldn't believe what she just heard. "So you lied to me about that too?"

April cut her eyes over to Zora and let out a heavy breath, ignoring her question. "You's a stupid bitch!"

"I fucking trusted you! And let's keep it a stack, your little foot business would have never lifted off the ground, not even an inch if I didn't set it up! All you did was had an idea with no way of putting it into action." Zora continued unleashing.

The tension in the room exploded into chaos.

"You needed me bitch! You and that sick trick were lost! If I didn't step in and come to y'all's rescue, you would have been selling pussy on the pavement!"

As April's tirade continued, Felicio locked eyes with Zora, their unspoken connection holding steadfast in the face of the storm.

It was then that Felicio took a deep breath and tried a different approach.

"You really need to seek help," Felicio told April in a calm, concerned tone. "If stuff doesn't go the way you have it set up in your mind, you'll do anything you can to tear it down. You fell in love with me and when it wasn't returned you tore me down, even exploited my past by making me relive it in the harshest way possible." Felicio shook her head as the memories came into focus again.

"Get over yourself, I'm over you."

"Then why you tearing up right now," Zora asked.

Felicio took another deep breath and walked closer toward April.

She wiped her tears away.

"Look, despite what's happened, I'm sorry for my part in all of this shit." Felicio admitted. "I should've tried harder to reach you when you kept shooting your shot, or at the very least, offered to help you. And the way I handled the Spades game because of it was just wrong." Felicio continued. "If I could go back, I would change everything." Felicio searched April's expression to see if her words were being received. "But I can't."

She couldn't tell.

"And guess what, it ain't too late, April. I'm here and I'm telling you, you about to lose everyone you love if you continue like this. It ain't worth it!"

Zora focused on April hard, hoping she would come around.

Silence hung in the air for a brief moment.

"Get the fuck out of my face!" April yelled. "Now!"

"Are you sure?" Felicio said. "Because once I'm gone there won't be a chance to get shit back."

"Get-The-Fuck-Ooouuuuuuttttttt!" April yelled.

Felicio walked to the door and Zora walked behind her. Whispering Felicio said, "Are you sure you're going to be okay here?"

"No...but for now I'll stay to figure shit out."

"I'll hit you back in a few days. To check on you." She pointed at her softly. "Make sure you take my call."

Zora hugged her tightly and Felicio walked away. She was halfway to the street when Zora came bolting out.

"Felicio!"

Turning around, she met her friend by the apartment. "What's wrong?"

"I'm leaving."

"Leaving? What happened that quick?"

"She offered me some tea."

"And?" She shrugged.

"I asked her to drink it first and she tossed it out."

Felicio took one step back and looked up at April who was glaring down at them from the living room window. "Yeah, it's time for you to bounce."

They both continued to walk down the street.

Apologizing and trying to make amends with April gave Felicio a sense of relief. She felt as if a huge weight had been lifted off her shoulders.

Crazy or not.

She couldn't control how April received it, but just knowing that she admitted her wrong doings and was done beefing with that girl left her with contempt.

She just hoped and prayed April could find what it was that she searched for before she hurt anyone else.

But she was done with the bitch.

PARKING LOT

Sitting in Felicio's truck that she had recently gotten back, Zora turned to her and asked, "So, what's your plan?" Her eyes searching hers for a glimmer of direction. "What do you want for your life?"

"What you saying for real?"

"Let me start by asking if you and Chanel are finally together."

Felicio paused, her gaze shifting from Zora to the chaos that unfolded around them.

She realized that she had been living day by day, surviving rather than thriving. But in that moment, with Zora's question lingering in the air, something stirred within her.

"Officially, we not together but I feel like it may be something there to possibly pursue."

Zora felt some kind of way. "Don't she got a nigga?"

"Too much to talk about." She sighed. "I *will* tell you that I don't have a clear plan," Felicio admitted. "I've been taking things day by day. But maybe it's time for a change. Maybe it's time to find something to strive for, something to build towards."

Zora reached out, her hand gently grasping Felicio's, a silent affirmation of solidarity. "Then let's figure it out together," she said, determination evident in her voice. "Let's navigate this uncertain path hand in hand."

"I don't have no money. Chanel's business not up and running yet, so I'm still on my dick."

"When I said figure it out together, that's what the fuck I meant. I got money, at least enough to keep us going until we know what's next."

Felicio's heart swelled with gratitude, and she pulled Zora into a tight embrace. They sat amidst the fuckery and broken friendships, re-bonded.

They pulled off the lot with hope for the future in their heart.

Meanwhile, April watched from the window as they drove away together with hate in hers.

COMING SOON

By C. WASH

The Cartel Publications Order Form
www.thecartelpublications.com

Inmates **ONLY** receive novels for $12.00 per book **PLUS** shipping fee **PER BOOK.**

(Mail Order **MUST** come from inmate directly to receive discount)

Shyt List 1	_____	$15.00
Shyt List 2	_____	$15.00
Shyt List 3	_____	$15.00
Shyt List 4	_____	$15.00
Shyt List 5	_____	$15.00
Shyt List 6	_____	$15.00
Pitbulls In A Skirt	_____	$15.00
Pitbulls In A Skirt 2	_____	$15.00
Pitbulls In A Skirt 3	_____	$15.00
Pitbulls In A Skirt 4	_____	$15.00
Pitbulls In A Skirt 5	_____	$15.00
Victoria's Secret	_____	$15.00
Poison 1	_____	$15.00
Poison 2	_____	$15.00
Hell Razor Honeys	_____	$15.00
Hell Razor Honeys 2	_____	$15.00
A Hustler's Son	_____	$15.00
A Hustler's Son 2	_____	$15.00
Black and Ugly	_____	$15.00
Black and Ugly As Ever	_____	$15.00
Ms Wayne & The Queens of DC **(LGBTQ+)**	_____	$15.00
Black And The Ugliest	_____	$15.00
Year Of The Crackmom	_____	$15.00
Deadheads	_____	$15.00
The Face That Launched A Thousand Bullets	_____	$15.00
The Unusual Suspects	_____	$15.00
Paid In Blood	_____	$15.00
Raunchy	_____	$15.00
Raunchy 2	_____	$15.00
Raunchy 3	_____	$15.00
Mad Maxxx (4th Book Raunchy Series)	_____	$15.00
Quita's Dayscare Center	_____	$15.00
Quita's Dayscare Center 2	_____	$15.00
Pretty Kings	_____	$15.00
Pretty Kings 2	_____	$15.00
Pretty Kings 3	_____	$15.00
Pretty Kings 4	_____	$15.00
Silence Of The Nine	_____	$15.00

Silence Of The Nine 2	$15.00
Silence Of The Nine 3	$15.00
Prison Throne	$15.00
Drunk & Hot Girls	$15.00
Hersband Material **(LGBTQ+)**	$15.00
The End: How To Write A Bestselling Novel In 30 Days (Non-Fiction Guide)	$15.00
Upscale Kittens	$15.00
Wake & Bake Boys	$15.00
Young & Dumb	$15.00
Young & Dumb 2: Vyce's Getback	$15.00
Tranny 911 **(LGBTQ+)**	$15.00
Tranny 911: Dixie's Rise **(LGBTQ+)**	$15.00
First Comes Love, Then Comes Murder	$15.00
Luxury Tax	$15.00
The Lying King	$15.00
Crazy Kind Of Love	$15.00
Goon	$15.00
And They Call Me God	$15.00
The Ungrateful Bastards	$15.00
Lipstick Dom **(LGBTQ+)**	$15.00
A School of Dolls **(LGBTQ+)**	$15.00
Hoetic Justice	$15.00
KALI: Raunchy Relived (5th Book in Raunchy Series)	$15.00
Skeezers	$15.00
Skeezers 2	$15.00
You Kissed Me, Now I Own You	$15.00
Nefarious	$15.00
Redbone 3: The Rise of The Fold	$15.00
The Fold (4th Redbone Book)	$15.00
Clown Niggas	$15.00
The One You Shouldn't Trust	$15.00
The WHORE The Wind Blew My Way	$15.00
She Brings The Worst Kind	$15.00
The House That Crack Built	$15.00
The House That Crack Built 2	15.00
The House That Crack Built 3	$15.00
The House That Crack Built 4	$15.00
Level Up **(LGBTQ+)**	$15.00
Villains: It's Savage Season	$15.00
Gay For My Bae **(LGBTQ+)**	$15.00
War	$15.00
War 2: All Hell Breaks Loose	$15.00
War 3: The Land Of The Lou's	$15.00
War 4: Skull Island	$15.00
War 5: Karma	$15.00
War 6: Envy	$15.00
War 7: Pink Cotton	$15.00
Madjesty vs. Jayden (Novella)	$8.99
You Left Me No Choice	$15.00
Truce – A War Saga (War 8)	$15.00
Ask The Streets For Mercy	$15.00
Truce 2 (War 9)	$15.00
An Ace and Walid Very, Very Bad Christmas (War 10)	$15.00
Truce 3 – The Sins of The Fathers (War 11)	$15.00
Truce 4: The Finale (War 12)	$15.00
Treason	$20.00
Treason 2	$20.00

By C. WASH

Hersband Material 2 **(LGBTQ+)** _____	$15.00
The Gods Of Everything Else (War 13) _____	$15.00
The Gods Of Everything Else 2 (War 14) _____	$15.00
Treason 3 _____	$15.99
An Ugly Girl's Diary _____	$15.99
The Gods Of Everything Else 3 (War 15) _____	$15.99
An Ugly Girl's Diary 2 _____	$19.99
King Dom **(LGBTQ+)** _____	$19.99

(**Redbone 1** & **2** are **NOT** Cartel Publications novels and if **ordered** the cost is **FULL** price of $16.00 **each plus shipping.** **No Exceptions**.)

Please add **$7.00** for shipping and handling fees for up to **(2) BOOKS PER ORDER**. (INMATES INCLUDED) (See next page for details)

The Cartel Publications * P.O. BOX 486 OWINGS MILLS MD 21117

Name: _____

Address: _____

City/State: _____

Contact/Email: _____

Please allow 10-15 BUSINESS days Before shipping.

PLEASE NOTE DUE TO **COVID-19** SOME ORDERS MAY TAKE UP TO **3 WEEKS OR LONGER BEFORE** THEY SHIP

The Cartel Publications is **NOT** responsible for **Prison Orders** rejected!

NO RETURNS and NO REFUNDS
NO PERSONAL CHECKS ACCEPTED
STAMPS NO LONGER ACCEPTED

CPSIA information can be obtained
at www.ICGtesting.com
Printed in the USA
BVHW031655030723
666729BV00007B/162